# DISHING UP

# DEATH

# DISHING UP DEATH

# Marie Celine

Beachfront Publishing

Beachfront Publishing, POB 811922, Boca Raton, FL 33481. Correspond with Beachfront via email at: info@beachfrontentertainment.com

First edition February 2005

Library of Congress Cataloging-in-Publication Data

Celine, Marie. date
  Dishing Up Death / Marie Celine
  p. cm.
  ISBN: 1-892339-95-1
    1. Women cooks–Fiction. 2. Pet food industry – Fiction. 3. Pet owners – Crimes against – Fiction. Los Angeles (Calif.) – Fiction.
  I. Title

PS3603.E45D57 2005                    2004056800
813'.6–dc 22

Printed in the United States of America

# DISHING UP

# DEATH

# 1

"Come on, Rich, let's get out of here." Fang Danson flung his cigarette butt across the room. It was a quick flash of orange, a tiny meteor hurtling across the dance floor, and then it was gone. Stamped out beneath the stamping feet.

"What?" The pounding disco music rattled Rich Evan's ears. He was buzzing. A night of drinking could still do that to him, though it took more and more alcohol to get his attention, let alone push him over the top.

"I said, come on. Let's go!" Fang drew the last word out like he was playing out a fishing line. His accent betrayed his London origins much more strongly than his mate's.

Rich nodded and headed for the door. Wobbling, bobbing faces waving and shouting farewell. They exited the club and the sudden relative quiet of Sunset Boulevard struck them like a blow.

"Ouch." Rich winced. The club had been all black lights and mirrored glass balls. The retro Disco Den was a current fave of the 'in crowd'.

"You gonna make it home?" Fang, six-foot two inches, skinny as a proverbial rail, with a head of carefully concocted blond curls, was shifting on bent knees. He fished for his car keys. They fell from his hand to the smelly pavement, grown filthy through the endless parade of Hollywood's unwashed masses. He stooped to retrieve them and some punk in a passing car shouted out an obscenity. Fang straightened and shouted back, as was his custom.

Rich laughed. "Too early to go home." He looked up the street. "Think I'll look for some action." He raised an eyebrow as if daring Fang to ante up.

Fang folded and waved his friend off. "Not me. I'm in the studio tomorrow. Got six sides to cut." With only moderate difficulty, Fang managed to crank up his Aston Martin.

Rich Evan giggled. Three young women were just leaving the Disco Den. A whiff of smoke and a belch of disco music accompanied them. They headed up the sidewalk. Rich followed.

So what if there were three of them.

It was a start.

He ran after them and jumped into their path. "Hello, hello, ladies."

They looked at him, blank and silent.

"Do you know who I am?"

The lead girl shook her head and said tartly, "No, should I?"

"Yes, you should. I'm Rich Evan." He waited for the ooohs and ahhhs. None followed. "Lead singer of Infinity Machine?" Still nothing.

Finally a second girl, a malnourished looking brunette with jeans hanging low on her hips, spoke up. "Oh my god, I know who you are." She turned to her friends. "Do you know who this is?"

Her girlfriends were still shaking their heads.

"He's this old rock guy. My mom and dad listen to his old records sometimes. They even play his music on that old rock station my parents make us listen to in the car."

Rich winced. That was three times the damn girl had used the word *old* in reference to him. He was only forty-seven for crying out loud. He forced himself to ignore the obviously unintended insult. "Are you girls up for a party?"

The lead girl's eyebrows shot up. She was the prettiest of the bunch and looked like a beach bunny. "With you?"

Rich nodded, desire creeping into his eyes.

The three girls laughed and, holding hands, walked past him.

Rich opened his mouth to call them back, but decided to preserve his dignity. He turned round to find his car. It was up the street in a valet lot. A woman was watching him from the door of the club. She was a pale thing, standing in the shadow of the building's awning. She met his eye and held her ground. She said hello very softly. He'd almost missed it.

"Hi," he replied. He started down the sidewalk.

"Need some company?"

Rich froze midstep. Well, this night wasn't going to be a complete waste of time after all.

Kitty Karlyle laid the insulated bag on the kitchen table, unzipped the side and carefully set a prepared tray of food down on the table. "He-re, Benny. Here, Benny-Benny."

Kitty peeked behind the trash bin in the corner of the kitchen. This was Benny's favorite place to hide. But not today. She bit her cheek. "Now, where can you be, you naughty pup?"

Benny had left a warm and sticky present on the kitchen floor. As a gourmet pet chef, not a pet caregiver or walker—as she was sometimes forced to gently remind her clients— it was not in Kitty's job description to pick up after the little dickens, but she didn't feel right just leaving it there for Benny's owner to discover, perhaps too late and on the bottom of his foot. She grabbed a paper towel from the counter and scooped the mess into the trash.

Normally, the sound of her voice and the scent of his morning meal would send Benny to the kitchen in a flurry of paws that skidded over the red oak floor. Of course, this morning, he'd been naughty. Kitty wouldn't have held this against him, but he was only a puppy and probably didn't understand such things.

The accident might not have been the poor spaniel's fault anyway. It could be Mr. Evan's fault.

"What happened, Benny?" Kitty cried out. "Did Daddy forget to let you out this morning? It's okay," she cooed. "Come get your breakfast."

Kitty frowned. Not a peep. She crossed into the media room, following the sounds of a television. The widescreen set was on but no one was watching. Her cell phone went off and she checked the number on her screen. "Oh, no. Not

Mrs. Randall, not now."

Kitty answered the call, much as she hated to. Mrs. Randall, oblivious to anyone else's life or eardrum safety, was screaming. It seemed Mr. Cookie, her cat, wasn't eating.

"You've got to hurry," cried Mrs. Randall. "Hurry, Kitty. It's an emergency!"

Despite her misgivings, and there were many, Kitty promised she'd be right over. And that meant driving all the way from Malibu back to Beverly Hills. She groaned. This time of day, that could take an hour.

Kitty gave one more shout for Benny or Mr. Evan. Neither appeared. She practically flew out the door to her car.

"Daddy's home!" Rich Evan tossed his car keys into the sink and yawned. "Where are you, you little bugger?" He clapped his hands. There was no sign of Benny.

He glanced at his Rolex. It was too late to go to bed. And he was famished. He pulled open the fridge. Nothing edible looked interesting.

Turning, Rich caught sight of the tray on the breakfast table. "Well, well." He rubbed his hands delightedly. "What have we here?"

He leaned forward and sniffed. He recognized the tray as one of those belonging to Ms. Karlyle's Pet Gourmet firm. "Hmmm-mmmm."

Rich looked under his feet for the dog. There was no sign of him. "Well, you little bugger, if you're not hungry, I am."

With that, he removed the foil revealing a tender bit of lamb mixed with some rice and vegetables. And was that a hint of saffron he detected?

He fondled the unlined index-sized card that always accompanied the dog's dishes. "Dog eats better than I do," he muttered as he read.

Kitty Karlyle Gourmet Pet Chef
—Benny Had A Little Lamb—

1 cup lamb, braised
½ cup finely chopped baby carrots
½ cup finely chopped spinach
1 cup brown rice, steamed
pinch kosher salt
hint of saffron

"Saffron, I knew it." The aging rocker was pleased with himself. All that coke snorting hadn't ruined his nose. How remarkable. He grabbed a fork from the drawer and dug in. The dish had a decidedly nutty flavor, though he couldn't place the variety.

Rich Evan yawned. Damn he was tired. And his throat felt sore. He hoped he wasn't coming down with something.

He helped himself to another delicious bite. He shrugged off his bodily complaints as the toll one must pay for another all too late night. It was a bit difficult to breathe though. Perhaps he'd catch a nap after he finished eating.

As Kitty dashed up the sidewalk, Mrs. Randall pulled open the door. Mr. Cookie, a sleek Siamese with cunning eyes lay stretched out in her arms.

"It's about time," Mrs. Randall said.

Kitty caught her breath and gave the cat a friendly swipe along the head. "Good afternoon, Mr. Cookie. What's going on? Not hungry today?"

"He hasn't touched his breakfast."

"I don't understand, I made him a breakfast steak and egg burrito. That's one of his favorites."

"Well," sniffed Mrs. Randall, of the Randall department store chain, "he hasn't touched a thing, I can assure you. If you don't believe me, see for yourself."

She swept the main door open and Kitty hurried inside. The Randall residence was one of Beverly Hills' most imposing with a veritable museum's worth of antique collectibles filling the halls and lining the walls.

Even the automobiles, and there were a great many in the garage, were antiques. Mr. Randall himself drove an old Mercedes to the office every morning which was so lovingly looked after by his full-time auto mechanic that it appeared factory fresh.

In the dining room, Kitty carefully lifted Mr. Cookie's silver tray from the marble floor. The food looked all right. She sniffed. "It smells fine."

She picked up the burrito. "It's cold. Perhaps if I warm it up?"

Mrs. Randall very nearly sneered. "Perhaps." Mrs. Randall closely followed Kitty to the kitchen.

Kitty had started to slip the steak and egg burrito into the microwave but, fortunately, caught herself in the nick of time. Mr. Cookie didn't like microwaved food. That would have been a huge faux pas and she couldn't afford to lose Mrs. Randall. Mr. Cookie was a twice a day customer. Breakfast and dinner.

She carefully warmed the burrito up in a cast iron pan over the humongous gas stove. To tempt Mr. Cookie further, she opened up the burrito, adding some freshly grated Romano cheese to the mixture. She took a pinch in her fingers and rolled it over her tongue. "This ought to do the trick."

"It had better, Miss Karlyle," Mrs. Randall said haughtily, still carrying the fidgety feline. "It had very well better."

Kitty held her breath as Mrs. Randall set the cat down on the small wooden table in the kitchen. This was where the help ate. Kitty placed the burrito back on Mr. Cookie's Wedgewood plate on Mr. Cookie's silver tray and ever so gently scooted the tray under his nose.

Mr. Cookie looked at Mrs. Randall, who looked most concerned. He looked next at Kitty. Kitty wordlessly screamed for him to eat. He sat back on his haunches, licked his whiskers, sniffed the air. . .

And ate.

Kitty sighed. Success! "Well, all's well that ends well. Right Mrs. Randall?" She smiled at the old woman. The old woman wasn't smiling back. That wasn't the way this was supposed to work.

Mrs. Randall's steely voice rang out. "At what hour will you be back to prepare Mr. Cookie's dinner, Miss Karlyle?"

"Six o'clock. Same as always, Mrs. Randall, ma'am." Kitty found herself fawning. She couldn't help it with Mrs. Randall. The woman had some sort of spell on her.

"Right, see that you are punctual. Mr. Cookie likes to dine on time. If he gets off his schedule it does terrible things to his digestion." She rubbed Mr. Cookie's tummy as he chowed down, delicately picking away at his breakfast burrito. "Doesn't it, Mr. Cookie?"

Mr. Cookie glanced up at Mrs. Randall, licked his lips and returned to his meal. When Mrs. Randall turned, Kitty was gone. "Well, I never—"

Kitty raced to her car, an old Volvo station wagon—so old it might have been a prototype—and hurried on her way. She still had one more trip to make back up in Sherman Oaks and that was to Ira and Iris Rabinowitz's house. She glanced at the backseat, hoping that Goldie's own dishes weren't getting cold. Being strict practitioners of their faith, the Rabinowitz's insisted that Goldie be on a traditional Jewish diet, and kosher only, of course.

After taking care of the Rabinowitz's dog, Kitty still had to drive back to her own apartment in L.A.'s Melrose district and prepare dinner for Mr. Cookie, Benny, and two other pets under her care. What with Mrs. Randall's emergency, her schedule was going to be tight—tighter than usual.

Kitty was in her element now, quietly and efficiently preparing meals for her clients' pets. The day's troubles forgotten, she loaded up her various meals in warming trays and filled the station wagon. This took three trips.

The sun was headed over the Pacific now, giving the sky that red glow that always made Kitty smile. She'd go to Mr. Evan's house first, as always, then work her way back into the city.

She pulled into the mansion's drive, the sound of the ocean carried through. There was a chill in the air here. The beach was always so much cooler than the valley. To this day, this always took her by surprise.

Climbing out of the Volvo, Kitty rubbed her arms, wishing she'd brought a sweater along. Carefully removing Benny's meal from the back of the vehicle, she made her way around to the side entrance, just off the kitchen. Out on the beach, she spotted a couple holding hands. Must be nice, she thought.

She heard a bark at the door and opened it. Benny came tumbling out, all paws and tongue. "Well, hungry now, are we, Benny?" She scratched his nose. "What's that?" She cupped her hand around her ear. "What's for dinner, you ask?"

Kitty rose, and said teasingly, "Well, we'll just have to see now, won't we?" She pushed open the door with her foot, balanced the warming tray in her hands. She could barely see in front of her nose. "Mr. Evan?"

There was no reply. "Mr. Evan, it's me, Kitty. I've got Benny's dinner." She shrugged. Kitty was used to eccentric clients. And living in Los Angeles, everyone knew that went with the turf. Rich Evan was as eccentric as they came.

Once she'd come to bring dinner and discovered the rocker in the media room standing on his head naked listening to Beach Boys music, zoinked out of his brains. Another time, she'd found him naked on the kitchen floor with four young girls, including one mother and daughter, being boinked out of his mind.

That had been something. Kitty still got red in the face

just thinking about it. "Looks like it's just us, Benny." She maneuvered through the narrow doorway.

"Careful," she said as Benny zigzagged between her feet. "Let's not have an accident."

Benny barked madly.

"Okay, okay, hold your horses, pup." Steering out of the corners of her eyes, she reached the island counter and set down the dinner tray. Benny's barking was beginning to give her a headache.

"Okay, okay." Kitty unzipped the insulated bag and pulled out the tray. She turned. "Here you g—"

Rich Evan lay face down at the kitchen table, his pale face nestled in a bowl of *Benny Had A Little Lamb*.

# 2

"WHAT DID YOU DO?"

Kitty turned. Benny was still yapping at her heels. A woman was screaming at her. She looked frightened. Wait, despite the distorted face and gaping mouth, Kitty recognized the howling woman. It was Consuelo, Mr. Evan's housekeeper.

Kitty was frightened, too. Did she look as awful as Consuelo? Because Consuelo was looking like Bela Legosi was about to take a bite out of her tender exposed neck.

Consuelo yelled at Benny to be quiet. When Benny wouldn't obey, she chased him from the kitchen and shut him in the laundry room. His muffled roar continued.

"You are the pet food señora." Her shaky finger pointed accusingly at Kitty. "What's happened? What did you do to Señor Evan?"

Kitty stood over Rich Evan's body. He didn't look good. In fact, he looked quite dead. Kitty had seen dead before and this looked like dead. Of course, the only dead she had seen before had been pets. And those had been goldfish.

Though Rich Evan wasn't floating belly-up in a two quart fish bowl, he looked unquestionably dead.

She looked at Mr. Evan's pasty face and limp, dangling arms. And there was that turtle once, a red-eared slider. His neck drooped when she'd discovered him dead. Rich Evan's neck drooped like that now.

And in Benny's breakfast to boot.

"I didn't do anything. I walked in only a minute ago and found him like this." Kitty's voice had an appeal to it that she hadn't intended. It was just that the housekeeper was even now picking up the telephone and calling the police. "Geez, Consuelo, do you think I murdered the poor guy or something?"

"Help!" cried Consuelo into the telephone. "Come quickly, please. It's my employer, Mr. Evan, and he is dead!" She gave the address and dropped the phone.

"We don't know that he's dead." Kitty held her breath and knelt closer to the body. One eye was half-open. Ugh. "Maybe he's only passed out."

"Don't touch anything!" shouted Consuelo.

"It's probably an overdose." Rich Evan liked to party hard and everyone in town knew this. The rocker was a frequent tabloid target. Kitty took one placating step in Consuelo's direction.

The housekeeper was fast. In one quick movement, she'd managed to cross the kitchen floor, wrest an ugly looking butcher's knife from the block on the counter and now was waving the dangerous looking blade in the direction of Kitty's nose.

Kitty sighed and waited for the police to arrive. She wondered how she'd look without a nose. Because the way that nervous housekeeper was waving that knife around, Kitty Karlyle wouldn't be stopping to smell the roses much longer. She regretted not having sniffed them earlier. There'd even been some rose bushes along the wall between Mr. Evan's garage and the house. Oh well.

Shouldn't one of the local community colleges offer a course on Smell The Roses 101? People would be much better prepared for the eventual snipping off of their noses or loss of their lives.

The sound of sirens echoing between the canyons of the mansions routed Kitty from a reverie she knew bordered on insanity.

The door burst open and an officer of the law burst in. His hand was wrapped tightly around the grip of a gun.

Kitty had a feeling Mrs. Randall was not going to take this well. Mr. Cookie's dinner was looking like it might arrive late, if at all. One client had just dropped dead and another was about to fire her. Kitty quickly calculated just how short she was going to come up on the month's rent. It wasn't pretty.

"Oh well," she muttered between tight lips, "that's the way the cookie crumbles."

Consuelo was pointing the butcher knife at her. The deputy was looking at her. "What did you say, miss?"

Kitty's mouth formed an O. No words came forth. She tried again, taking a deep, relaxing breath before she began.

"My name is Katherine Karlyle. I work for Mr. Evan." She nodded towards the body. "He was like that when I came in."

Consuelo started up a stream of Spanish that stopped only when the deputy laid his hands on her. The good thing was, from Kitty's perspective, that he'd taken her knife away and dropped it on the kitchen counter well out of the quick-triggered housekeeper's reach.

"You want to repeat that in English, miss?"

Consuelo aimed her finger in Kitty's direction this time. Her fingernails looked sharp but nowhere near as deadly as that steel blade. "She said she murdered Mr. Evan!"

Kitty's neck snapped. "I did not!" She turned to the deputy who by this time had company. Three officers were now looking at her like she was some sort of a criminal. "I didn't," she protested. "I only asked Consuelo if she thought I murdered him."

The third and youngest looking deputy, who would have been cute in any other circumstance, stepped towards Kitty and read her her rights.

"This can't be happening." Kitty shook her head.

"You understand your rights, miss?"

"Yes, of course I do. But I didn't *do* anything." She cast a nervous look at the middle officer, the oldest looking of the trio, as he examined Rich Evan.

"Dead all right," declared the officer.

It seemed to Kitty that there had been a touch of excitement in his voice. Maybe this was his first case involving a dead body.

Consuelo gasped and made the sign of the cross.

"Are you sure?" Kitty laid a hand on her chest. Had that

squeak come from her?

He nodded. And he looked serious. Dead serious.

Like a scene from a bad movie, the room filled with crime scene investigators and street cops. Kitty had never seen so many guns in one place. Throw in a couple of bazookas and these guys could conquer Catalina Island.

A man in a blue suit took Consuelo aside. Another fellow in a brown suit with black loafers asked Kitty to step into the media room. Maybe he was looking for a fashion consultant. If so, Kitty had some suggestions for him.

He asked her to sit and she chose an ottoman next to the black leather Sharper Image massage chair. Kitty had tried that chair once at Rich Evan's insistence. She had to admit it had felt good, but in an unnerving sort of way.

The chair had seemed to be getting way too personal with her. The half-alive thing had gotten all the way to second base before she had leapt out of the seat to the sounds of Rich Evan's hysterical, baritone laughter.

These days she preferred the ottoman. Though the way her sex life was going, maybe a massage chair wasn't a bad idea.

The brown suited man extended a lightly browned hand. "Detective Jack Young. And you are?"

Kitty shook his hand. His palm was warm. "Katherine Karlyle."

Det. Young pulled a narrow notebook from his inside jacket pocket and scribbled. "Are you the cook?"

He was looking at Kitty's outfit. Her hand rubbed her collar. She had on white slacks, low heeled white sandals and a white chef's coat. Kitty felt it was important to look professional when serving her clients. "That's right." She squirmed. "Though I prefer the term 'chef.' "

Det. Young shook his head and sighed. "Fine. So, you're Rich Evan's *chef*—"

"No."

"No? No what?"

Kitty stood. "No, I am not Mr. Evan's chef."

"But you just said—"

"Oh, I understand."

"I'm glad someone does."

"Don't you get it? You asked me if I was the cook and I said that I was and that I really preferred chef, because I did attend culinary school and prefer to be called a chef and—"

Det. Young cut her off. "If you don't mind, Ms. Karlyle, I have a dead body chilling in the next room and don't have a lot of spare time right now." He looked at her crossly. "What is your point?"

"My point, detective, is that I am not Mr. Evan's chef."

Det. Young squeezed his temples, leaving red blotches where his fingers had tried to access his skull. "You're not?"

"No, I'm Benny's chef."

Det. Young cocked his head. "I see." He tapped his pencil against his pad in an arrhythmic tempo. "Does Benny live here with Mr. Evan?"

Kitty nodded.

"Good. I'd like a word with him."

Kitty put a hand to her lips to squelch a laugh.

"Something funny, miss?"

"No, nothing's funny. It's just—" How was she going to word this? "You can't exactly talk to Benny. I mean, you can talk to him but he can't answer, not exactly, that is. Not with words."

Young's eyes narrowed. "You didn't kill him, too, did you?"

"No!" Kitty pointed. "He's in there."

"Show me."

Kitty went to the laundry room and opened the door slowly. Benny came racing out. He took one look at all the strangers and began barking like a Tommy gun. She picked him up. "Oh, you poor thing. You're trembling."

Young scooted past girl and dog and peered into the laundry room. Washing machine, dryer, cabinets, sink, drain, ironing board. No Benny. "So, where's this Benny fellow?"

Kitty held the puppy up in the detective's face. Benny licked him good, from his lower lip to the tip of his nose.

"Hey!" Young wiped his face off.

"Sorry," Kitty said.

Young stared at the dog. "That's Benny?"

Kitty gave Benny's paw a little wave.

"You're a *dog* cook?"

# 3

Kitty drew herself up. "I am a gourmet pet chef."

Young laughed.

Kitty glowered and lowered Benny to the floor. "I don't see what is so very funny. You don't see me making fun of your job, after all."

"That's because I've got a real one," Young replied with a smirk.

"Oh, good, a cop with a sense of humor. I'm sure poor Mr. Evan appreciates that a whole bunch. Don't you think so?"

"Listen, *chef*, I'm simply trying to do my job and I would appreciate a little cooperation from you. I'm sure," Young said, tapping his notebook with the wet eraser end of his pencil while Benny sniffed at his loafers, "that Rich Evan would appreciate that."

"I am being cooperative," countered Kitty. "At least I'm trying to be. If you would only let me tell my story—"

The detective sighed. "Fine, let's go back in the other room and sit down. You talk, I'll listen."

True to his word, the detective kept his mouth shut and his notebook open long enough for Kitty to spill her whole and mostly unembellished story. She slapped her hands against her knees. "And that's what happened." She leaned closer. "My guess is a drug overdose."

"A drug overdose?"

Kitty raised a telling eyebrow. "You know how rock stars are."

"No, do tell."

"Well, I'm not saying it's true of all of them, but Mr. Evan certainly was found of—" she wanted to phrase this nicely, "pharmaceuticals."

"Pharma—Oh, you mean drugs. Pot, coke, that sort of thing?"

Kitty nodded. "I could tell you stories."

"I'm sure you could."

Kitty wasn't sure how he meant that, good or bad. It sounded downright sarcastic. "It might even have been a heart attack. All that partying Mr. Evan did, it could have taken quite a toll on his health."

"So you're an MD as well as a dog cook, Ms. Karlyle?"

Kitty rose. "I'm only trying to help, detective."

"And we at the L.A. Sheriff's Department appreciate it, miss. But we have a medical examiner all our own." Young glanced at the victim who was even now being packaged for delivery. "I'm sure he'll give us a cause of death." His eyes bored into Kitty. "And we'll take it from there."

His look sent shivers up her spine. Why did she feel so guilty? She hadn't done anything. Kitty looked at her watch. Mrs. Randall was going to kill her. "Can I go now?"

Det. Young flipped back through his notepad, and repeated Kitty's address and phone number out loud. "Is that correct?"

Kitty nodded.

"We'll be in touch."


Kitty raced across the lawn to her car. "Aarrgh!" She clenched her fists and groaned in frustration. "Boxed in!" Official vehicles were all over the property and spilling out into the street.

She had to beg a young uniformed cop to help her out. Late as she was, Kitty stopped at a favorite little pet shop she frequented and picked up a frozen treat for Mr. Cookie—a box of Goodlicks Catcicles in assorted flavors.

With the box of frozen dessert treats under her arm and Mr. Cookie's dinner in her hands, Kitty loped up the Randall drive. The houseman answered the side door.

Kitty glanced at the stern looking, sharply dressed man and asked, "Is the coast clear? Has Mrs. Randall been asking for me?"

The houseman, Gil Major, cleared his throat in a most civilized fashion. He was a most civilized, British born and trained servant who had just reached that age where the AARP would be after him. He'd also now be eligible for the Senior PGA Tour, though with that stiff back of his Kitty couldn't imagine how the man could ever lean over far enough to reach the ball, let alone hit it.

"The missuz was called out. Mr. Randall telephoned and asked her to meet him at the Four Seasons for dinner."

Kitty let out a sigh of relief. "Thank goodness." She dodged past Gil to the kitchen, popped the frozen treats in the deep freeze and pulled out Mr. Cookie's not-so-warm evening entree.

Even though Mrs. Randall was nowhere near, Kitty followed her ritual to the letter. She laid out the Wedgewood as she called to Mr. Cookie and gently laid out his omelette. The card read:

*Kitty Karlyle Gourmet Pet Chef*
*—Mr. Cookie's Jack and Dill—*

2 eggs, lightly beaten

1/8 cup skim milk

1/4 cup salmon, steamed

1/4 cup Monterrey Jack, grated

pinch kosher salt

pinch dill

Mr. Cookie hopped onto the table and dove into his dinner. Kitty smiled. It was always nice to feel appreciated. She scooped up her hotpack and waved goodbye to Gil.

She'd made it onto the back stoop when a shrill alarm went off in her head. What if there was something wrong with the *Jack and Dill?*

What if she poisoned Mr. Cookie?

Kitty turned swiftly about and raced to the kitchen. Mr. Cookie was halfway through the omelette. Gil was feeding the darn cat out of his hand.

Kitty reached for Gil and yanked his arm away. "No. Stop!" she cried.

Gil gasped and pulled back. Mr. Cookie made a run for it, disappearing in the direction of the formal dining room.

"That was close." Kitty scooped up the plate and slid the remains of the omelette into the garbage disposal.

Gil was looking angrily at his jacket.

Kitty felt something in her left hand and slowly opened her fingers. A button. She looked at Gil's sleeve. A strand of thread hung loose. "Oops." She smiled wanly. "Sorry about that. But don't worry, I can sew it up for you."

She reached for Gil. "Why don't you give me your coat and I'll fix it up good as new and bring it back tomorrow. I'm pretty good with a needle and thread."

If there is a tomorrow, she thought glumly. If Mr. Cookie dropped dead from her cooking, tomorrow would be Mr. Cookie's funeral quickly followed by her own.

He drew back protectively. "That will not be necessary, Miss Karlyle." The houseman looked at her crossly. She felt her cheeks burn. "Whatever were you thinking?"

"I-I was afraid that the omelette might not be fresh. I was running late, as you know, and well. . ." Kitty refused to meet his gaze. "Maybe I could whip up something here in the kitchen?" She pulled open the Sub-Zero. "Yes, I see loads of possibilities."

Gil pushed the door closed. "That will not be necessary,

Miss Karlyle. I'm sure that Mr. Cookie has had quite enough."

"Yes," said Kitty, crestfallen, "I suppose he has." Mrs. Randall had probably had enough too. "Do you think I could say goodbye, I mean, goodnight to Mr. Cookie?"

Gil pointed to the door.

Back in her apartment, Kitty racked her brain. What had happened to Rich Evan? The TV ran in the background. Every so often CNN popped in something about the rock star's death. But there had been nothing to explain how he had died.

Had she poisoned Rich Evan?

Had she poisoned Mr. Cookie?

Kitty thought of all the other pets she'd fed that day. Were they dead or dying even now? There had been no horrified messages on her answering machine from irate pet owners, so perhaps not.

Then again, just because their pets all died, her clients might not have pieced together yet that she had somehow been responsible.

Just as she thought her friend Velma would never arrive, the doorbell rang. Kitty threw open the door. "Velma, thank goodness!"

Velma Humphries, known as 'The Hump' throughout high school, had been Kitty's bestfriend since they'd gone through the Culinary Institute of San Diego together. Velma gave Kitty a squeeze. Being a large woman, this was often tough on the recipient's ribs.

"You look a little sunburned," commented Kitty, stifling

a groan.

"Working in the garden. That's what I get for letting it go so long."

Kitty nodded. Velma loved her garden. Kitty often wished she had as many interests to occupy her life as her friend did. Velma was not only an excellent chef, she was an expert gardener and even pretty good with computers. "You should have worn a hat. I haven't seen you this red since you came back from Hawaii."

"Yeah." Velma took Kitty's hand. "Forget about me. Are you okay? I heard some more about it on the radio on my way over."

"Yes, I'm fine. Thanks for coming." Not knowing what else to do, Kitty had called Velma and dumped her troubles on her. It was either that or call her parents down in Newport Beach. No thanks. They'd find out soon enough, she feared.

"No problem." Velma sashayed over to the sofa. Her purple mou-mou hid a good third of the green cushions. She looked like a giant eggplant floating in a pool of guacamole. "So, tell me all about it, you poor thing."

Kitty spilled her guts. When she finished, she asked, "What do you think I should do?"

"Nothing."

"Nothing?"

"That's right. Look, all we know is that Rich Evan is dead. It doesn't have anything to do with you. You're no killer."

"But what if there was something wrong with my food?"

"Is there? I mean, you haven't killed Fred and Barney, have you?"

Kitty shook her head. "No, last I checked they were sleeping on my bed." Fred was Kitty's black Lab and Barney was a stray black and white pussycat who'd taken up residence in her apartment as well. It was a good thing the landlord had a policy that, while not strictly allowing pets, for the most part, tolerated them.

He tolerated people, too, though just barely.

"Have you checked the icebox for anything suspicious?"

Kitty looked toward the kitchen. "No, I haven't dared. Not yet."

Velma pushed off from the couch and opened the fridge. She scooped up a carton of milk, eggs, assorted meats and cheeses and dumped them all in the trash can under Kitty's sink.

"What are you doing?"

"Getting rid of all this." Velma reached into the refrigerator for seconds.

"But we haven't even checked it all out yet. What if something is bad?"

Velma laid her hands on Kitty's shoulders. "Listen, Kitty, if any of this food is tainted, you can't use it. It's garbage." She removed practically everything from the refrigerator, leaving nothing but an open box of baking soda and the butter.

"But the police might want to—"

"To what? Search your apartment to see if any of this stuff is contaminated? They'll tell you to destroy it if it is. All we're doing is saving them the trouble." Velma neatly tied up the bagful of food and hauled it out the door. "Be right back after I feed Mr. Dumpster."

Kitty watched her friend go. It didn't seem right throwing all that food away. Not only was it a waste and a strain on her already broken budget, but if something she'd prepared had been the cause of Rich Evan's death it didn't seem right throwing away the possible evidence.

Velma returned empty-handed. "That's that."

"I'm still not sure about this. I mean, even if I did poison Mr. Evan, it was an accident—"

"Will you forget about it, already?" Velma sat Kitty down at the kitchen table. "If the police had anymore interest in talking to you they'd be here already."

"You think so?"

"I know so. Katherine Karlyle is no killer, accidental or otherwise." Velma reached out and patted her friend's hand. "My guess is that the cops have already figured this one out. Guys like Rich Evan drop dead all the time. If the booze doesn't get them, the drugs do. The coroner's report is bound to clear you. You'll see. This whole thing is going to blow over like a summer shower."

"I hope you're right, Velma."

Velma smiled. "I'm always right."

# 4

First thing the next morning, Kitty headed to Ralph's, Trader Joe's and Mrs. Gooch's, in that order. Her food supply needed replenishing. As she slid her Mastercard through the little electronic box at Gooch's, she realized her credit was in serious need of replenishing as well. She wasn't going to be able to keep charging forever.

Kitty was drowning in a mountain of debt.

Kitty pulled at her watch, hoping it was running fast and knowing that it wasn't. She herself was running late. She whipped up something quick for Fred and Barney while she prepared more elaborate meals for her clients' pets. Of course, today there would be one less client to worry about.

"Wait," she said aloud, "what am I thinking? Just because poor Mr. Evan is dead, I can't let little Benny starve." She grabbed her pencil and decided on one of Benny's favorites:

*Green Bean Eggs and Ham.*

The door rattled.

"Come in," called Kitty, spatula in hand. It was probably one of the guys next door. Five young men, all members of some struggling rock band, called The Tonsils, were crammed like sardines into the one-bedroom apartment next door. Whenever one of them caught wind of Kitty's cooking. . .

The door shook again.

"I said 'come in'!"

The door slowly opened.

Kitty dropped her spatula. It sizzled with the sliced ham in the cast iron pan. "Oh, it's you."

"Good morning. Det. Young, LASD."

Fred ran up, sniffed the detective's shoes, seemed satisfied and went back to his post in front of the stove, waiting not so patiently for handouts or accidents. Barney raced out the door for parts unknown.

"I remember. What do you want? Ouch!" Kitty removed the spatula, licked her fingers and turned the ham. Afterward, she went to work chopping green beans which she planned on steaming. But time was in short supply so she'd have to heat them up in the pan. "I'm kind of busy here."

"I can see that." Det. Young was poking his nose into her grocery bags, some paper and some plastic, which were lined up across the kitchen counter. He gingerly pulled up a deboned tuna wrapped in plastic. "Been shopping?"

Kitty glanced up from her cooking. "What do you want?"

"I thought you might want to know how the investigation into Rich Evan's death was going. He was your client after all."

29

"Was it a heart attack?"

The detective shook his head.

"What then? Drugs? It was drugs, wasn't it? Like I said." She sighed. "Poor Mr. Evan."

"It wasn't drugs. At least," said Young, "not directly. Things are up in the air. I've just heard a preliminary report." He grinned. "Go ahead, guess again."

Kitty stopped her chopping and wiped her hands on her apron. The detective was smirking. She hated smirkers. And she wasn't about to give him the satisfaction of taking his bait.

After a moment of stalemate, Det. Young said, "It appears that Rich Evan may have had a close encounter with a deadly substance."

A deadly substance? Kitty blanched. "You mean. . . ?"

Young nodded.

All her fears had come true. She'd sweated through the night, tossing and fretting, praying that Velma would be right and that Mr. Evan's death had nothing to do with her or her cooking.

"The ME seems pretty certain it was something he ingested. We'll know soon enough."

Kitty turned off the stove. She poured herself a glass of water from the sink which was usually the last place in the world she'd drink from. She drank the cool water down in one awkward gulp.

"What I don't get is why would this Rich Evan character be eating dog food? I mean, you said you cooked for the dog, not him." The detective leaned over the pan of seared ham and sniffed. "Smells good. I haven't had my breakfast yet."

Kitty pulled the pan off the stovetop. "Sorry, this is for my customers. And what I feed Benny isn't exactly dog food. I use the finest ingredients. My food is not something you simply dump out of a can. There's nothing in my meals that a person couldn't eat if he or she chose. Not that I've ever known Mr. Evan to eat Benny's food before."

Young shook his head. "You always feed dogs this good?"

Kitty pulled a carton of eggs from the Gooch's bag and broke two into a bowl. "And cats, and pigs, birds and reptiles."

Young laughed. "I get it. Whatever they pay you for."

"That's right."

He popped a raw green bean over his tongue. "And you go to people's houses and you cook for these things?"

"That's pets. And, yes, I do. If you had pets, you'd know how people, *caring* people, look after their pets. We consider ourselves caretakers, not owners."

"As a matter of fact, Miss Bleeding Heart, I do have a pet."

"Oh?"

"That's right, a dog. A black lab. Like yours."

"Oh." That had caught her by surprise. She regrouped and fired back. "I bet you feed the poor thing out of a can."

"The poor thing has a name and it's Libby. And, yes, I do. Got a problem with that?"

"No, not as long as you eat out of the same can."

"Funny. You're real funny. Maybe you should be a pet standup comedienne."

Kitty checked the flame and poured the eggs into an eight

inch pan. "Why not? If the police can afford to pay a detective to do standup comedy like you do, I suppose I could find someone to pay me to do the same for their pets."

Young reached down and petted Fred. "So, how much do you charge for preparing meals?"

"That's none of your business."

"I don't know about that." He scratched Fred behind the left ear. "Maybe you're right. Maybe I'll hire you to come and cook up some gourmet treats for Libby."

Kitty looked the detective in the eye. "Thirty dollars for once a day, fifty for twice."

Young whistled. "You're kidding?" He scratched his head. "A guy could buy a lot of Alpo for those kind of bucks."

Kitty finished up and set about preparing to leave on her daily rounds. "Are we finished?"

Young's voice turned serious. "We are going to need to confiscate your food."

"You want to know if anything is contaminated."

"That's right."

"Don't you need a warrant for that?" Kitty knew she shouldn't be giving the detective a hard time but he was so infuriating, she couldn't help herself.

"Do I need one?"

Kitty sighed. "No. Look, I already thought about this. That's why I went shopping this morning. I didn't want to take any chances. If there was anything wrong with the food, it was an accident. I still don't believe it though. Still, Velma took it all, everything that was in the fridge, and threw it in the dumpster."

"Velma?"

"One of my friends. She said I shouldn't take any chances on the food being tainted."

"Well, she's right. But then again, that food needs to be tested. You should have called before throwing it out. That could be evidence."

"I'm sure it's still out there." Kitty pointed. "The dumpster is down in the back of the parking garage. They don't pick up until Thursday."

But she didn't get away from Det. Young that easily. He made her accompany him to the dumpster, identify her trashbags and help him carry them back up to his car. The stink was incredible. She hoped it stayed with him all day, with his car, too.

Before driving off, Young said, "Tell me, Ms. Karlyle, if you're Benny's chef, why did you leave the food on the kitchen table? I'd say Benny's a little short to eat from a chair."

Kitty went over her movements once again. "I told you yesterday. When I got to Mr. Evan's house, no one was around. I let myself in and set out Benny's plate. I called him and he didn't come. He'd had an accident on the floor. So I thought he was only hiding because he knew he might be in trouble. Dogs can sense it.

"And then my cellphone rang and it was Mrs. Randall having a fit because Mr. Cookie wasn't eating." Kitty shrugged. "I raced out of there. I left the plate on the table, I suppose, without thinking."

She looked into the distance. "It's my fault, isn't it, that Mr. Evan is dead?"

Young backed up his car. "When I come to that conclusion," he said grimly, "you'll be the first to know."

Kitty stood, letting the morning sun beat down on her. Some days it felt so light. Today it was a heavy, onerous weight hanging over her head. Det. Young had said 'when' not 'if.'

# 5

"Calm down," replied Velma. "Even if it does turn out to be food poisoning and the police can prove that it's the food you had prepared for Benny, it's still only an accident. An unfortunate accident."

Kitty nodded but she wasn't assuaged. This was more than just an unfortunate accident. Rich Evan was dead and there was a good chance she had killed him. "I have to go, Velma." There was a small space across from the house and she managed to parallel park. "I'm at the Rabinowitz's."

Mr. and Mrs. Rabinowitz were all comforting hands and words of sympathy. They made Kitty sit down on the sofa in the living room and tell them all about it.

By the time she pulled free and fed their plump little Pekingese, Goldie, her brunch, *Goldie Lox and the Three Bears*, Kitty was running late once again.

Benny was going to be her next stop, though it was out of the way. She wondered how the little pup was doing without his master.

Pulling up to the pitch-roofed gatehouse of the decidedly un-Hollywood-like Malibu Colony entry, Kitty wondered whether the guard would even allow her to enter, given what had occurred the day before. But, after painting her with a somewhat odd and questioning look, he let her pass without a word.

Kitty sighed with relief. Now if only Consuelo, who was bound to be up at the beach house, would just not start screaming at the top of her lungs the minute she arrived, point her finger and brand her a murderess, this day might not turn out so badly.

The Evan home was located on Malibu Colony Road. A yellow Ferrari was at the edge of the driveway. Kitty wondered whom it belonged to. It wasn't Mr. Evan's. The driver's side window was open and a cigarette smoldered in the ashtray.

Consuelo was in the kitchen sweeping up. One hand held a green-handled, nylon bristled broom and the other a gray metal dustpan. Kitty was gladdened to see this left no hand free for a lethal weapon, pointed or otherwise.

The housekeeper looked up as Kitty gingerly crossed the kitchen threshold. "Oh, it's you."

Kitty said hello. "I brought Benny some food. I thought he might need it." She looked about. "Where is he?"

"I'm only sweeping up. Like always. It's impossible to keep the sand out of this house. Stupid to live at the beach, if you ask me."

Kitty nodded obligingly. She set Benny's meal on the granite-topped island. "Have you seen Benny, Consuelo? I don't want his food getting cold."

Consuelo rolled her eyes. "That puppy is around somewhere. Probably following Mr. Danson about."

"Mr. Danson?"

"Mr. Danson is Mr. Evan's friend." Consuelo looked briefly at Kitty then returned to her sweeping.

The woman sure didn't seem too shook up today about Mr. Evan's passing. It briefly crossed Kitty's mind that Consuelo herself might have done her employer in. The way she wielded that knife, Kitty wouldn't put it past her. Consuelo was as volatile as a jug of nitro.

And Kitty sure wouldn't turn her back on the woman again, especially in a room full of cutlery. Still, what motive might Consuelo have had for murdering her employer? Might he have provoked her?

Recipe:

Take one volatile Mexican with a flare for knife wielding.

Add one crazed and sometimes obnoxious rock star.

Stir briskly.

Result:

One less rock star?

Kitty called softly to Benny. He wasn't in the media room or out on the back patio watching the surf which she knew he was fond of doing. Benny often took his meals out on the redwood deck. The doors were open. Kitty helped herself to a breath full of luscious, life affirming sea air. It was another bright, sunny day in sunny southern California.

Too bad Rich Evan wasn't around to enjoy it.

Kitty followed the sound of rustling papers and found a tall, gaunt looking man with an unruly head of brown hair, riffling through the desk in Mr. Evan's office. Benny was at the man's feet. The puppy ran to Kitty and she bent down to pet him.

The man dropped the papers and glared at her. "Who are you?"

"I-I'm Katherine Karlyle. I brought Benny his food."

The tall man pushed the desk drawer shut, slowly and thoughtfully. His hard green eyes seemed to penetrate her skin. "Fine. Just leave it in the kitchen, will you. I'll take it with me when I leave."

Kitty began to retreat then stopped at the door. "But I'm afraid his meal will get cold. He really ought to eat now."

The man's eyebrows pinched together. He snapped his fingers and his dour countenance brightened considerably. "Oh, I know who you are. You're that chef girl that Rich recently hired to cook for his doggy."

Kitty nodded.

The man came out from behind the desk and introduced himself. "I'm Fang Danson."

"Katherine Karlyle. Everybody calls me Kitty though."

"How appropriate." Rich's eyes darkened. "I hear from the police that it might have been your cooking that did old Rich in."

Kitty didn't know what to say. After all, he could be right.

"Look, I was going to take Benny home with me. Rich would have wanted it, I'm sure." He bent low and ruffled the pup's coat. "Why don't you go feed Benny and then we'll be off."

After the girl and the dog left, Fang returned to his friend's desk. He'd made a pretty good search of it and turned up nothing. Nothing but a baggy containing about an ounce of hash. He'd stuffed that in his pocket. What the hell. It was better than leaving empty-handed.

Sitting in Rich's chair, he dialed a number from memory. "Yeah, this is Danson. I'm at Rich's house and there's nothing here. Nothing that I can find anyway. I thought you told me he had the papers?"

The voice on the other end told him not to worry.

"That's easy for you to say." Fang dropped the phone in its cradle.

He found the girl sitting cross-legged on the kitchen floor, Benny between her legs, scarfing up something that smelled awfully good. Looked good, too. So did that cozy spot between the girl's legs. She was a looker, despite the cook's getup.

She glanced up as he came into the room. Fang smiled. What had she said her name was? Katherine? Cat? Kitty, that was it. "He looks happy." Fang showed his teeth.

Benny's tail waggled back and forth as he ate. "Yes. Still, I feel terrible. I mean, what if the food I prepared yesterday was bad somehow? It was meant for him. Benny could be dead right now," she said softly. "And poor Mr. Evan. . ." Her voice trailed off.

Fang dropped to his knees beside the girl and laid a comforting arm over her shoulder. "Don't you worry none.

It's not your fault, Kitty. Rich, he had a good run of it." She was looking at him now. There was hope in those eyes. "The way I hear it, he went without any pain. A fella can't ask for much more than that."

She was surprised to find she was crying again. Fang grabbed a paper towel and handed it to her. "Sorry," she said.

Fang helped the shaken girl to her feet. "Listen, Benny needs you. And I can see he likes you. You take good care of him," Fang said smoothly. "Benny's going to be staying with me now. I want you to continue cooking for him."

"You do?" Her eyes cleared a little.

"Absolutely. Benny needs you." Fang stared into her light blue eyes. "I need you. I've never had a dog before. I wouldn't begin to know what to feed him. I'd probably go out and buy some bag of kibble or something."

Kitty looked aghast. She couldn't help herself.

"You see?"

"Well—" She did love Benny, but seeing the little pup only served to remind her of Rich Evan's death and how close Benny himself might have come to being killed by her hand; accidental though it might be. She was beginning to wonder if this whole pet gourmet business was a mistake. Maybe she should give it up altogether?

"For Benny's sake?"

Benny had finished eating and was barking to be let out. Consuelo, who'd been dawdling over a few dirty glasses in the sink, sent him on his way.

Maybe, Kitty thought, if she helped take care of Benny, it would atone some little bit for whatever responsibility she might have had in his owner's death. "Okay. But I won't charge you. I can't take any money for it. This is on me."

"We'll worry about that later." Fang scratched out his address on the back of one of Kitty's business cards. Kitty promised to bring Benny his dinner later that same day.

Making her way back to the station wagon, Kitty spotted Fang Danson with his arms around a knockout of a young woman in a blue leotard and jogging shoes. Her hair was long, flowing and naturally blonde. Kitty had always wanted hair like that. Heck, she'd always wanted thighs like that. The woman had the looks of a Hollywood starlet.

Fang released the young woman and drove off.

Consuelo was emptying her dustbin in the trashcan along the side of the garage.

Kitty approached her. Hands open. "Who was that woman?"

"What woman?" Consuelo's eyes were suspicious and wary.

"The one in the drive that Mr. Danson was talking to."

Consuelo practically growled. "That was Mrs. Evan."

"Mrs. Evan?"

"Yes, the former Mrs. Evan. Angela Evan. Mr. Evan, he divorced her." She shook her head. "I was happy. I did not like that woman."

"What do you suppose she was doing here?"

"She lives here in the Colony also." Consuelo left Kitty standing there and retreated to the house.

Benny was running around the yard. Kitty went to him and picked him up in her arms. "Say, little guy. I thought Mr. Danson was supposed to be taking you?" She frowned. Danson was long gone. She scratched Benny's tummy.

"Looks like he forgot." What should she do? She didn't really want to leave the helpless puppy at Mr. Evan's house, not in the care of Consuelo. "I guess you'll have to come with me."

Kitty carried Benny to the car and told him he could ride shotgun. "You can be my assistant for the rest of the day."

Heading back up through the Colony towards Pacific Coast Highway, Kitty noticed Mrs. Evan walking briskly on the side of the street. Her arms swung side to side like a pro's. One hand clutched a cellphone.

Kitty pulled up alongside.

The blonde stopped. There wasn't a drop of sweat on her. Up close now, Kitty looked her up and down. There wasn't so much as an ounce of fat on her either, except for those regions men found irresistible.

"Can I help you?" Mrs. Evan seemed to look at Kitty's old car and immediately put her in her place. The driver of this car was 'the help' not a peer. The blonde's chest rose and fell confidently and serenely.

Kitty was trying awfully hard not to hate her. "Mrs. Evan?"

"What do you want?" The woman's eyes were teal colored and marble hard.

Kitty took the woman's reply for a yes. "I wanted to say that I'm sorry to hear about your ex-husband's death."

Mrs. Evan half-smiled. "Richie is my husband—was my husband." Her eyes darted up to the distant Malibu hills. "Yes, it's a shame. Now, if you don't mind, I really must be going."

"Yes, of course," Kitty said. Benny took this moment to stick his head out the window and yap.

"What are you doing with that dog?" demanded Mrs. Evan.

"This is Benny, Mr. Evan's dog."

The blonde frowned. "I know what the thing is." Benny leaned out the window and she awkwardly patted his snout. Her fingers came back gooey. She frowned, then wiped her hand on the side of her leg, leaving a long silvery streak, like a snail's trail which she tried unsuccessfully to rub out. "What are you doing with him?"

Kitty explained.

The more she explained the more Mrs. Evan's eyes narrowed and her soft body stiffened. "You're the chef Richie hired."

"That's right. Katherine Karlyle." She reached for her purse which was on the floorboards. She fished about. "I've got some cards here someplace."

"That really isn't necessary. I am not a pet person."

Kitty didn't think the woman was much of a people person either.

"The way I hear it, it was your cooking that killed Richie. Maybe I should be thanking you. My dear husband was a real bastard."

"I beg your pardon?"

"Serves him right being poisoned to death eating dog food."

A stunning young brunette in salmon-colored sweatpants and a matching bikini top jogged up and patted Mrs. Evan's arm. "What's up?"

"Nothing," said Mrs. Evan. She turned her back on Kitty and Benny and went running off with her girlfriend.

"Be grateful you're not going home with that woman, little guy." Benny barked. Kitty took this as the dog's way of expressing his agreement.

# 6

"So there's no doubt?" Det. Young held the phone pressed up between his ear and his left shoulder. His hands were busy applying glue to the left front fender of the scale model Porsche 359 spread out across his desk.

"No doubt at all."

"That's tough," said Young, and he meant it. That Karlyle girl, though goofy beyond a doubt, had seemed like a nice girl. Cute, too. "Thanks, doc. What was the name of that stuff again?"

The doctor happily repeated his results.

"The Barbados nut. Spell that for me." He dropped the fender and scratched down the name. "Got it." He ended the call and reattached the fender, holding on a good minute until it had had time to affix itself to the front body. So Rich Evan had been poisoned. That dish he'd eaten had been laced with

Barbados nut.

According to the ME, the stuff was lethal and had once been used by veterinarians as a purgative. Hell Oil, he'd called it. That explained the diarrhea the victim had suffered on his way out of this world. The detective had come across a lot of ugly ways to go in his career, and this was one of the ugliest. To top it off there were traces of multiple illicit drugs in Evan's bloodstream.

The man had been a walking high school chemistry experiment. That combined with the Barbados nut had made a potent and lethal combination.

But was it murder or stupidity combined with carelessness? In this town, you saw both.

Young made a mental note to himself to research this Barbados nut later. Right now he was going to have to figure out whether this Karlyle woman had killed Evan on purpose or by accident.

Was she a nut herself? Had she set out to kill Rich Evan? Maybe she had intended to murder the dog? Maybe she considered herself a chef who practiced a little euthanasia on the side?

Young resealed his glue pen. Now that he knew what he was looking for, he would order the lab to search the food he'd retrieved from Karlyle's dumpster and check it for this Barbados nut.

He'd have to have a second word with the Karlyle woman, too. And he wanted to take a look at that recipe. He found her phone number in his notebook and gave her a ring. She wasn't home or wasn't answering.

True to her word, Kitty arrived at Fang Danson's manse around seven-thirty that evening. She was exhausted. It had been a nightmare of a day, running around, preparing meals, taking care of her own pets, Fred and Barney, while dragging Benny along everywhere she went. Of course, he'd had to stay in the car when she was servicing her other clients' animals.

The dog, like all puppies, was a never-ending swirl of paws, legs, tail and tongue. Even now, he twisted in her arms as she rang the front bell. The chime was playing a piece that Kitty identified as something by Edvard Grieg. Those youthful hours lost to piano studies hadn't been totally wasted.

Fang Danson's Santa Monica home was a modernistic, three-storied palace, white with a blue tile roof, standing out among the smaller homes on the quiet street where he lived. The garage was open and Kitty couldn't help but notice the yellow Ferrari, along with a blue Aston Martin and a metallic black Rolls Royce. There were also two motorcycles and a racing bike.

Fang answered the door himself. He was in loose jeans that hung off his bony hips. The jeans were torn at the knees and the floppy white T-shirt was wrinkled and had brown stains. Danson was barefoot as he stepped out on the Chicago brick porch. For a moment, it didn't look like he recognized her. "Oh, you've brought the dog," he said finally.

Kitty held out the puppy. Fang took him and set him down. Benny ran off sniffing the bushes.

Kitty adjusted her toque. Her chef's coat was covered with dog hair. She held out her hand. "Good evening, Mr.

Danson. Yes, I brought Benny as I promised. I have his dinner in the car. I hope it's not too late."

"Nah. Day's just begun. Come on in." He turned and disappeared inside.

Kitty stared at the open door. "Wait right here, Benny, while I go get din-din."

Framed gold and platinum albums adorned the walls of the high-ceilinged entryway. So, Fang Danson was a rock star also? Funny, she'd never heard of him. She read off the names of his records silently. They were all by one band: Milky Way. Of course, they'd been huge in the seventies and eighties, producing album-oriented rock along with their peers like Pink Floyd and the Alan Parsons Project.

"Surprised?"

Kitty turned. Fang stood behind her, his hands in his pockets.

"Me and the boys didn't like to tour. We considered ourselves more a studio band. I like to stay home with my toys."

Kitty nodded. He seemed to have a lot of toys, expensive toys. "I really love your music."

"Thanks." Fang sniffed the air. "That smells good." He reached over and unzipped the warming bag she carried. "This is for the dog?"

"Yes." He was smiling but something about the man frightened her.

"What is it?"

"I call it *Peas Porridge*."

Fang scrunched up his nose. "What?"

"See?" Kitty pulled the small white card from her pocket

and handed this to Fang.

He read, "Peas Porridge. Fresh peas, minced chicken breast, diced shitake mushroom, whole milk, one-quarter teaspoon cod-liver oil . . ." Fang made a face before continuing. "Sea salt and fresh pepper."

"Where shall I feed Benny?"

Fang shrugged. "Wherever you like."

"The kitchen?"

"Kitchen's through there." He pointed down a long hall leading to the right. At the end of the hall, a bright light protruded. Kitty and Benny headed this way.

Fang disappeared up to the second floor. A hand reached out and pulled him into his expansive and professionally outfitted home recording studio.

"What on earth is *she* doing here?"

Fang kissed the woman on the neck. "Relax. Nothing to be jealous about, love. The girl's only here to feed the dog."

The woman shook her head. "I'm not jealous, you idiot. I don't like it, that's all. There's something about that girl that rubs me the wrong way."

Fang could think of plenty of ways that Kitty could rub him and none of them were wrong. "How do you mean? Besides, I wasn't even aware that you knew her."

Fang turned to the recording console where he'd been mixing down some tracks and rechecked his levels. Today's session had gone well and with luck the new album would be out in three months tops. Now if those record promoters he was paying a bundle to could only get some airplay. Not easy in this day's tight-arsed, cookie-cutter, youth-driven market.

"She stopped me on the street this morning to tell me how sorry she was about Richie's death."

"We're all sorry." Fang nestled up behind and squeezed her buttocks. "Relax, Angela. So she stopped to give you her condolences. The girl's a kook, I mean, got herself a job feeding cats and doggies, but there's nothing peculiar about her saying how sorry she was about your ex's death."

Angela pushed up against Fang, leaned back and caressed his chin. "Well, I still don't like her. I know her type. She looks like trouble to me."

"And you look like trouble to me," Fang said, lustily, as he spun Angela around and pushed her down atop the chenille sofa along the back wall.

Halfway into things, Angela came up for breath and managed to say, "What about that girl? She's downstairs, for Heaven's sake."

Fang grinned and removed Angela's pants in a smooth and practiced move. "Good thing this room is sound-proofed." He kissed her hard. "A girl could scream here if she wanted to. And no one would hear."

"Mr. Danson?" Kitty poked her head out the hall. Where had he disappeared to? She'd finished feeding Benny. The pup was sleeping it off in a corner of the kitchen, near the back door.

All she wanted to do now was go over her arrangement with Mr. Danson, work out a schedule of feedings, et cetera, and she could be on her way. Kitty yawned loudly. A good night's sleep was the only thing she needed after that.

Kitty searched the entire first story. There was no sign of

Mr. Danson.

She left a note for him on the kitchen counter explaining that she would be back first thing in the morning to feed Benny his breakfast.

She let herself out the front door.

Det. Young was waiting outside her building.

Kitty ignored him as she unlocked the door to her apartment. He followed her inside.

She wearily set her supplies down on the sofa. Fred came running and leapt into her lap. "How's my baby?" She stroked his back. Barney mewled from the kitchen. Kitty looked at Det. Young. He had wandered back to the bedroom, apparently casing the place.

Kitty stood and went after him. "Are you going to tell me what you're doing here, detective, or am I supposed to guess? Because if I'm supposed to guess, I'm afraid you are going to be very disappointed, because I am very tired." She folded her arms and blocked the hall.

"I was hoping to get a recipe."

"A recipe?"

"That's right. For that *Benny Had A Little Lamb* stuff of yours."

Kitty's eyes narrowed. "Why?"

He shrugged. "Curious, that's all."

Kitty turned her back on him and went to the kitchen. Her fingers scanned through her recipe file. She had her entire collection on index cards in a small box near the stove. She whipped out the recipe in question and thrust it into Young's hand.

He read it over.

"Satisfied?"

"No Barbados nut?"

"Excuse me." Kitty found some leftovers in the fridge from the meals she'd prepared that morning and laid out plates for Fred and Barney. They ate greedily.

"No Barbados nut." He flicked the index card. "The recipe doesn't call for any Barbados nut."

Kitty smirked. "Don't tell me. You're a chef now as well as a detective and a comedian." She shook her head. "So now you're going to tell me how to cook, is that it?"

Young carefully laid the index card on the counter. "No, that's not it at all. I had a call today."

"Lucky you." Kitty prepared herself a cup of hot tea. "Care for some?"

"Thanks."

Kitty prepared two cups of herbal blend sweetened with blueberry honey.

They carried their cups to the sofa.

Det. Young took a sip and set his cup on the floor. Fred stuck his nose in it once then took off. "That call was from the coroner's office. Rich Evan was definitely poisoned by the dish you'd prepared for his dog. No wonder he was lying face down on the plate."

Kitty froze, her cup suspended between her lap and her lips. She looked like one of those preserved corpses from Pompeii after the eruption of Mt. Vesuvius enshrined them in ash and lava.

Young seemed to be enjoying the look. "You know what they do down there at the ME's office?"

Kitty said nothing. Slowly she took a drink of her tea. This was like a bad movie.

"In the case of Rich Evan, they examine the contents of the victim's stomach. They found the undigested remains of Benny's intended dinner. Only this dish contained Barbados nut." The detective detailed the nut's poisonous properties with an apparent relish.

"But I never even heard of this Barbados nut!" Kitty pushed forward. Tea ran down her coat. The way the detective was looking at her was making her nervous. Did he expect her to crack? To confess?

"Then how do you explain it being in the meal you prepared?"

"I-I can't."

"There were traces of the nut on the dish still, in the uneaten remains."

Kitty stared straight ahead, avoiding his gaze, biting her lip. "I don't know. I can't. I mean, I prepared the food here like I always do. And then it was with me all day. I swear, I don't have any idea."

She was looking at Det. Young now. "Maybe it was some unlisted ingredient in something that I put in the food." Kitty was clutching at straws now and knew it. She ran through the ingredient list in her head. It didn't make sense. "The rice maybe?"

"We've checked everything out. Everything that we could find, that is." He stood and set down his empty cup. "We're going to need to search your apartment and your car."

"Now?"

He nodded. "I'll call and arrange a tow."

She blanched. "You're impounding my car?"

"I'm afraid so. But don't worry, if it's clean, you'll get it back soon enough."

"But I need it in the morning. I have meals to deliver."

"Sorry." He let himself out. "Thanks for the tea."

"Thanks for helping me out. Are you sure you won't get in trouble at work?"

Velma had a part-time job flipping burgers at a Jack-In-The-Box in Culver City, not far from the little studio-sized room she rented at the back of a small 1940's built home owned by a retired postal worker and her husband, himself a retired veteran who'd been on disability since being shot up in Belgium during WWII.

"Nah. Those jerks can get along without me for a day. Half the people who work there don't show up half the time. It's about time I took a little time off. I'm always covering for those jerks. Let's see how they like it for a change."

Velma dropped two insulated bags into the trunk of her car, adding to several others already piled there. She wiped her hands on her frock. "If we run out of room in here, I can clear some space on the backseat."

Velma's car was notoriously junk-filled. Velma always said that it was because she lived in such a small apartment, but she was only fooling herself. Velma was a hoarder. She'd have a brand new, stretch limo filled with junk inside of a week if you let her.

"I don't think that will be necessary. This is about everything." At least she hoped so.

"I really appreciate your coming with me and letting me use your car like this," Kitty said again as Velma headed up Melrose.

"Hey, stop thanking me. What are friends for?" She turned up towards Beverly Hills. "Besides, this is fun. It's kind of like old times."

Kitty nodded. She closed her eyes and enjoyed the cool morning breeze hitting her face. L.A. was beautiful this time of day. The air was crisp, the city vibrant with everyone scurrying here and there. It really was a bit like old times, like Velma said. Kitty and Velma were close. They had been classmates through the San Diego Culinary Institute.

Velma was from Michigan. She had been living in a house trailer in the woods behind her grandmother's house in St. Clair Shores. Her only work experience had been writing reviews for mystery novels and posting them on the Internet. Of course, for this she had received no pay as she had done it on her own. But it had given her something to do.

Except for writing up hundreds of reviews on mystery novels (most of which she rated bad) and old films (which she rather enjoyed), she had little to do besides feed herself and her cat (she'd had a cat then) and play the dulcimer. She wasn't a very good dulcimer player and the cat looked neglected and undernourished.

About the only thing Velma did well was criticize. That and grow. The adipose tissue grew around her as if providing a literal layer of insulation between herself and the world-at-large.

Velma had lived rent-free on her grandmother's rural property. Her parents were school teachers in the Detroit school system but she rarely saw them. They'd given up on their daughter as a lost cause—she'd barely graduated high school and immediately upon doing so had bought herself a dulcimer and locked herself in her room—and gave most of their attention to the troubled teens who passed through their high school classes believing their energies were best spent here.

After a few good blow-ups with her folks, Velma moved out in a huff and a puff—it was the most she'd exerted herself since ninth grade gym class when they'd been forced to attempt the Presidential Fitness program. Granny Humphries took her in.

Velma had been sleeping on Granny's porch after running away and had caused the spill in which Granny Humphries, whose eyesight wasn't what it used to be, tumbled from the front porch and busted her right hip on her way to the mailbox. But Granny had a good heart, and a new hip, and told her granddaughter that she could move into the tiny trailer out back that was just sitting empty since her last tenant had moved out as the FBI closed in. It seemed the previous renter had himself a small meth lab and knew his time had come.

Sitting around, slamming mystery novels and mesmerizing herself watching old films, growing rounder (her grandmother remarked to a neighbor that Velma ate enough cereal to keep Battle Creek on the map), strumming that cheap dulcimer, picking cat fur out of her mou-mous, that had been enough of a life for Velma Humphries and this was exactly how she had spent her first three years post-high school. She'd been known as The Hump in high school due to her slouched posture and zaftig status.

And while these teasing, taunting high schoolers were wrapping up three years of college and getting ready for the fourth and final, The Hump was sitting in her dump, as the teasers and taunters would say to one another whenever Humphries' name came up in a what-ever-happened-to sort of way.

Then one day, Velma had had an epiphany, or maybe it just came to her while watching the umpteenth rerun of the umpteenth episode of The Beverly Hillbillies. In any event, she dropped the cat at her grandmother's doorstep, 'borrowed' Granny's Chrysler and headed for Tinsel Town.

But Tinsel Town didn't want her and after a month she'd drifted down to San Diego. A flyer stuck in her windshield while she was carousing in a Lucky's grocery store announced the upcoming fourteen week semester at the San Diego Culinary Institute.

A quick reverse-the-charges phone call to Granny Humphries and her tuition was covered. Velma was in cooking school training to be a chef. It was exhilarating, exciting!

Hey, it was free. And she was surrounded by food! Life

was sweet and so were the pastries she'd be creating. Granny Humphries, in her own elation at Velma's sudden nose to the grindstone attitude, had even started sending her a monthly stipend.

Velma and Kitty soon ran into each other. They had places across the table from one another in a class on meat identification. The instructor, Pierre Durdus, was a tyrant who believed meat identification only second in importance to memorizing the Ten Commandments.

Velma and Kitty used to get drunk on the wine Velma was swiping from the Institute's kitchen, while they made up horrible dishes in which Chef Durdus was the main ingredient.

Velma even went so far as to write the most unusual recipes down. One such was Durdus au Jus; ingredients included one deboned Pierre Durdus, six gallons of mirepoix ( a mixture of chopped onions, celery, carrots, herbs and seasonings), a gallon of jug wine, and bell peppers (Durdus hated bell peppers).

Velma told Kitty they should write a cookbook. She said she had a lot of experience with books and knew the good from bad. As time went on, the odd duo went from classmates to roommates.

By the time they had both graduated some eighteen months later, Kitty had formed her idea of becoming a pet gourmet chef. Velma had aimed higher—and fallen lower. Then she had let Kitty talk her into moving back up to L.A. Kitty had her pet gourmet cooking business up and running. Velma was flipping burgers and churning fries at a Jack-In-The-Box.

Why Kitty didn't just break down and get them both jobs at her folks' upscale restaurant in Newport Beach was beyond her and Velma often said so. After all, Kitty's cutesy folks, Mark and Paula, kept saying the door was open—and that went for the both of them.

Kitty only shrugged and said that she and Velma would both feel better if they made it on their own.

"You'll see, Velma," Kitty would say. "One of these days, it's all going to come together for us. We'll be super successful. I'll have a dozen pet chefs working for me, taking care of the world's pampered poodles and you'll be running your own hoity-toity restaurant in Beverly Hills or maybe West L.A.."

In the meantime, Velma was chauffeuring Kitty around in an '86 LeBaron on permanent loan from Granny Humphries. And together they barely had gas money to see them across town.

The good times had better come soon.

The first stop was at the Bel Air home of two men that Kitty only knew as Richard and Timothy. They'd seen Kitty's flyer outside a Trader Joe's in Toluca Lake and given her a call.

The girls donned their chef smocks and caps. "You can wait in the car, if you like." Kitty checked her image reflected in the car window, a hand-smudged and duller version of her self.

"Nah, this will be fun." Velma popped the trunk and read the labels Kitty had stuck to the warming boxes. "All of these?"

Kitty nodded. "If you really think this is fun, you should

join me. I've said it before, we'd make a great team."

"No, thanks." Velma started for the front door of the manse, a grand early American masterpiece of red brick and white columns, or at least La-La Land's version thereof. And she wasn't ruling the whole place out as a prop until she got a closer look. This was the land of façades, after all, and that went for people as well as places. "Cooking for pets is your thing, not mine."

Velma had exactly zero interest in kowtowing to the upper class and their little beasties. "I'm holding out for a real job in a four-star restaurant or better."

Kitty had heard it all before. "Okay, okay. Just remember, the offer is always open." She called Velma back. "We'd better go this way."

Kitty directed Kitty's eyes to a small green sign that pointed around the side. On the sign was the word *staff* and an arrow aiming to the back of the house.

Velma frowned. "You see? This is exactly what I hate about this job." Nonetheless she took the redbrick path to the kitchen.

Kitty introduced herself to the cook who in turn called Richard and Timothy. Within moments, they came in from the garden. Timothy held a basket of pink and yellow flowers. Both men, whom she judged to be in their fifties, were tall and lean. Richard's hair was still brown and full though, where Timothy's blond hair was thin and graying.

Kitty went through her routine. She'd brought three dishes for the dogs to sample. Us and Them were two sleek, muscular Dalmatians, both male, both sporting diamond studded leather collars.

As Richard and Timothy had requested, all the eggs used were from free-range, cage-free hens and all the meats were organic, the vegetables too. Kitty had gone all out. She really needed some new clients. The demoed dishes included Bowser's Burritos, Dalmatian Delight (which was her workhorse chicken loaf dish) and Healthy Hotdog Delite, made with tofu sausages.

Richard and Timothy gleefully read the small menu/recipe cards that Kitty had included. "One-half cup of mixed veggies. . ." Richard raised an eyebrow in Kitty's direction.

"That's broccoli, cauliflower and carrots," she explained.

Richard went on. "One-half cup shredded Monterrey Jack cheese, two tablespoons of chopped cilantro, mmm-mmm." He cleared his throat. "One beef bouillon cube, one teaspoon of chile powder, a quarter of a cup of crushed pineapple, two medium-sized baked sweet potatoes, and two and a quarter tablespoons of soynut butter."

"Interesting," said Timothy. He set his flower basket on the counter.

Richard went on. "One clove of garlic, one pound of organic beef and a tablespoon and a half of safflower oil." He beamed. "Delicious."

The dogs ate everything up and looked at Kitty, their eyes filled with contentment and hope. Got any more? they seemed to ask.

Richard and Timothy were thoroughly delighted and signed up for the six day, twice daily service. Richard actually kissed Kitty on the cheek. "You are wonderful, Kitty," he exclaimed. "Isn't she wonderful, Timothy?"

Timothy, by far the quieter of the two gentlemen, agreed. "Do you do cockatiels?"

"Sure," Kitty quickly replied. "I can do that. I've got some great bird recipes."

"So have I," Velma uttered under her breath. "Cornbread stuffed, with aspic is always good. . ."

"What's that?" Richard asked.

"I said you're getting yourself the best chef money can buy." Velma blushed. "You can't go wrong with Kitty Karlyle's pet gourmet service."

Richard and Timothy nodded wholeheartedly. And Kitty agreed to start in earnest the next day.

As they loaded their wares back into the trunk, Velma said, "I cannot believe how much people are willing to pay you to cook for their pets. It's amazing." She slammed the lid down.

"It wouldn't surprise me," Velma said, as they headed up Stone Canyon Road, "if folks like that don't spend more on their pets than they do on other people."

"You know how it is," Kitty said, "this is Los Angeles. You can find everything here. There are pet astrologers, pet psychiatrists, psychologists." She smiled. "I've even seen advertisements for pet exercise studios."

Velma snorted and looked in Kitty's direction. Any day now, she expected to see a storefront open up offering Pet Taebo or Pet Pilates. As one of her favorites, W.C. Fields, would say, 'there's a sucker born every minute.'

By the time they arrived at Fang Danson's house for
Benny's evening meal, both girls were bushed. Velma
maneuvered the old Chrysler up the narrow drive and killed
the engine. She leaned back against the headrest and sighed.
"If you don't mind, I think I'll wait here."

Kitty nodded. "This won't take long." She carried Benny's
dinner, Hickory Dickory Duck, up to the house and rang the
bell. Edvard Grieg chimed her presence and Fang Danson
himself opened the door.

"Come on in," he said with a wicked grin. He was in
crumpled jeans, his feet were bare and he was shirtless. He
sniffed, his nostrils pulling wide. "Mmmm, dinner time."

"Where's Benny?" Kitty walked to the kitchen and began
pulling out the dog's dinner.

"Good question." Fang's head tilted to one side. "Must

be out back." He went to the kitchen window and looked outside.

Kitty followed suit. Fang Danson's yard was large by Santa Monica standards. There was even a pool and a hot tub with room left over. But there was no sign of the dog. "I don't see him."

Fang snapped his fingers. "Wait a minute, I think I saw him upstairs earlier. I'll bet the little dickens is messing around up there." He grabbed Kitty's hand. "Come on, let's have a look."

Kitty dropped the plate of Hickory Dickory Duck on the kitchen counter. "But, Mr. Danson, really I don't think I should—"

"Come on." Fang wasn't taking no for an answer and he held Kitty's hand as far as the stairs when she was finally able to wrestle her fingers free from his sticky grasp.

Nonetheless, Kitty followed Fang upstairs. He pushed open a door. "Not in the guest bath."

He led Kitty down a hall lined with more hit records and photos of himself and his bandmates with a host of other celebrities. There were a number of photos that included Rich Evan as well. Pangs of remorse and guilt stung Kitty's heart like killer bees as she passed each of these.

Fang turned, mischief dancing in his eyes. "You know, he might be in the bedroom. The little guy has taken a liking to sleeping on the bed."

Kitty hesitated at the threshold. Danson's master bedroom was a huge suite, all white, with a massive canopied bed with an intricately carved frame its centerpiece. A fluffy white satin comforter floated on top. The room even boasted a fireplace. A pile of neatly stacked logs looked ready to go. "I don't think Benny's here, Mr. Danson."

Fang's toes wriggled in the thick white carpet. "Call me Fang. All my friends call me Fang. Haven't I already told you that? Besides, I'm not big on formality." He took Kitty's hand again. "Let's check under the bed."

Kitty dropped to her knees and looked. "I don't see—" Fang dropped down behind her, up close and personal. Kitty reddened and jumped to her feet. "Mr. Danson!"

He laughed. "What? I thought we might have some fun."

Kitty quickly pushed her skirt down. "I barely know you."

"And I barely know you. What better way *to* get to know each other?"

"I thought we were looking for Benny?" Kitty's eyebrows came together. "You haven't lost him, have you?"

"No," grunted Fang. "Of course not. The little bastard's around here someplace." He looked meaningfully at the bed. "Are you sure you wouldn't like to—"

Kitty's arms were crossed over her chest and she was tapping her foot.

"No, I suppose not." Fang sighed. "Ah, well, I think he's in the studio. The bugger's been running around in there all day. Taken a liking to it for some reason. Come on."

Though dubious, Kitty followed Fang back down the hall. He pulled open a redwood door that had to be six inches thick and motioned for her to enter.

"Benny?" Kitty slowly took in the room. She stood in a large control room. On the other side of the glass, running the length of a futuristic looking recording console, was the recording booth, with a baby grand piano in one corner, microphones, music stands and cables crisscrossing a wooden floor.

She felt a whoosh of air as the door closed behind her. She turned. Fang locked his arms around her waist and dragged her to a sofa that she hadn't noticed when she'd stepped in.

He pressed his lips to hers. Kitty valiantly tried to push him off. But the man was nearly a foot taller than she and quite a bit heavier as well.

The door opened. Fang looked up in surprise. His hands, which only a moment ago had been groping Kitty, were now pushing hair from his face.

Kitty smiled. Velma stood in the doorway. In her extended arms she held Benny, a squirming tangle of puppy energy. Velma looked with interest at the scene on the sofa. "I found this little guy scratching away at the front door trying to get in. I knocked but nobody answered. I figured I'd better bring your pooch in before he ruined the door."

Kitty took this moment to push Fang off the couch.

He crashed to the floor. "Who the devil are you?"

Velma explained.

Fang was shaking his head. "No. That's not it. Don't I know you from somewhere?"

"That depends," Velma said.

"On what?"

"On how much you like Jack-In-The-Box." Velma winked at Kitty. Kitty had taken Benny and Benny seemed as glad to see her as she was to see Velma. Velma held out a hand. Fang took it and she helped him to his feet.

He dusted himself off. "If you ladies don't mind, I've got

some work to do. Why don't you take Benny downstairs and feed him." Fang turned his back on the girls, plopped himself down in a black leather chair on wheels at the console and began pushing levers.

Kitty and Velma gave Benny his dinner in the kitchen. "Thanks for saving me back there."

"It was nothing. That guy looks sort of creepy to me."

"I agree," said Kitty. "And I don't like the way he's taking care of Benny, or rather, not taking care of him. What was Benny doing running around outside unsupervised, anyway? He could have been lost or stolen. Maybe ended up in one of those awful labs where they experiment on poor, innocent creatures."

"Beats me."

"I'm not sure it's such a good idea for Mr. Danson to have Benny. He's really not very responsible, is he?" Kitty petted the puppy lovingly. "You poor thing."

"Why don't you just take him?" Velma whispered.

"What? You mean take Benny?"

"Sure," urged Velma. "That creep isn't going to give this little guy a good home. You take him."

"I can't do that. That would be wrong. Besides, I've already got two pets. I don't think the manager of my building would like it if I brought home a third. You want him?"

Velma picked up Benny's empty plate and stuffed it in the bag. "Can't have pets where I live, remember?"

Kitty's phone went off like an alarm. She answered on the third ring. It was Mrs. Randall. "Hello, Mrs. Randall. How are you this evening?"

"Not well at all, young lady. These reporter people are creating quite the nuisance." Mrs. Randall had said 'reporter' like it was a four-letter word.

"What reporter people?"

"The ones tramping all over my lawn wanting stories."

"What sort of stories?" Kitty was getting a sinking feeling in the pit of her stomach.

"Lurid and sensational stories. They want to know about you. And some man named Rich Evan that they say is dead." Mrs. Randall sighed in frustration. "There they go again ringing the bell. What are you going to do about this, Miss Karlyle?"

Kitty groaned. "But it's not my fault. What can I do about it?"

"You can come here and get rid of them," Mrs. Randall demanded.

"Get rid of them? How am I supposed to do that?" Kitty dropped her phone back in her purse. There was no point in waiting for an answer as Mrs. Randall had hung up.

Velma asked, "What was that all about?"

"Mrs. Randall. She says a bunch of reporters are asking questions about me and Mr. Evan. She wants me to get rid of them." Kitty shook her head. "How on earth am I going to do that?"

"Don't worry." Velma pushed Kitty out the side door. "We'll take care of them."

By the time they got to Beverly Hills, a small troop of pushy reporters had gathered around the Randall manse.

Kitty groaned. "I had no idea."

"You haven't been watching television much, have you?" replied Velma.

Kitty shook her head. "I haven't had time. I've been busy."

Velma shrugged and pulled over to the curb several houses away from the Randall residence. There were several news vans on the street. One had a long antenna sticking from its roof like it was expecting to contact aliens or something.

"Rich Evans was a pretty big celebrity. What did you expect?" Velma said, looking at Kitty whose eyes had grown as big as saucers, flying or otherwise.

Kitty looked around her, soaked it all in. She felt like she'd slipped into another world. Not the one she intended. Not the one she belonged in. Not the one she wanted to live in.

All she wanted was to earn a living cooking for a few pets. "I didn't expect all this."

Velma opened her door. "You stay here."

"What are you going to do?"

"They're reporters. I'm going to give them what they want."

Kitty's eyes narrowed. "What's that?"

"A story."

Velma walked towards the reporters who lingered about like well-dressed sharks on the sidewalk. She quickened her pace as she approached. "Help! Quick!"

Heads turned.

"You've got to call the police!" Velma cried. "I was

walking my dog—he's a Doberman Pinscher—on the next
street and," she huffed and leaned forward, her hands
clutching her knees, "he got away from me." Her eyes flicked
from face to face. "And he's mauling Robert Redford!" She
pointed.

The street cleared. As the vans shot past, Kitty heard
someone yelling at his partner to get his camera ready.
Interestingly, not one of the news crews had been overheard
mentioning calling the police or fetching an ambulance.

Velma wiped her hands and slowly walked back to the
car. There was a big grin on her face. "Reporters are so easy."

Despite her troubles, Kitty found Vel's smile infectious
and combined with Velma's bravado, this was enough to
make her laugh and went a long way towards lightening her
worried heart.

Kitty jumped out of the LeBaron. "I'd better go and have
a word with Mrs. Randall." Still, a frosting of reluctance
covered her words. "Why don't you come with me, Vel?"

"Nah. Think I'll wait here." Velma turned on the car
radio.

"Come on," urged Kitty, not wanting to face an angry
Mrs. Randall alone, "you were responsible for me getting
Mrs. Randall as my first client after all. Since we're here
anyway, the least you can do is say hi."

"That was Granny Humphries' doing."

"Sure," said Kitty, "but give yourself some credit. You
were the one who telephoned Granny Humphries and asked
her to refer my service to Mrs. Randall."

"Like I said at the time," Velma was fiddling with the
radio dial, "it's no big deal. Granny knew Mrs. Randall from

back in Mrs. Randall's Michigan days. Randall Department Stores started in Detroit, you know. Granny worked the perfume counter there for forty-five years."

Velma suspected that forty-five years of breathing in perfume and cologne fumes had addled Granny's brains, but as this addled state usually turned out in Velma's favor, she kept this opinion to herself. She still had the Chrysler, didn't she?

Granny was a free spirit and deserved her independence. It would be terrible for Granny to end up in a nursing home somewhere. She'd die if they stuck her in a place like that.

Kitty nodded. She'd heard the story before. Granny Humphries had joined with Randall when it was only the one small store in East Detroit. Granny Humphries had known Mrs. Randall personally and had generously telephoned her on Kitty's behalf. The Randalls had been Kitty's first, and to this day, were her most difficult, clients. And this included the recent addition of the all hands Fang Danson.

Her second client had been Rich Evan, whom the Randalls had subsequently referred. In the service industry, and very much so in L.A., word of mouth was key to success. People like Mr. Evan and the Randalls could make or break her.

Kitty tried once more. "Still, you know Mrs. Randall would love to meet you. You ought to come up and say hello, Velma. She'd be so glad."

"Another time maybe." Velma yawned. "These old bones are beat. I thought working a long shift on my feet in front of a fryer at Jack-In-The-Box was hard. I don't know how you can stand this; driving around L.A. and the Valley, back and forth and back and forth. Yo-yo city. Give me a warm spot in front of a Viking range in a five-star restaurant any day."

What could Kitty say? She knew how Velma felt, but she loved her job and wouldn't change it for anything. Kitty sighed. "I'll be back in a minute."

The front door opened even as her feet lighted on the porch. "It's about time you got here, Miss Karlyle." Mrs. Randall's sharp nose led the way.

"Good evening." Kitty forced a smile, though it was admittedly weak as watered down tea. "The reporters are gone, I see."

"Yes, finally. It has been most upsetting with them all malingering about, tramping all over our lawn. Mr. Vickers just planted petunias, you know. Most upsetting," she tut-tutted, "for all of us, including Mr. Cookie."

"I am so sorry. I can't imagine what they were doing here."

"I overheard one of them say they had been following *you*." Mrs. Randall's eyes were hard. "And since you had been here earlier feeding Mr. Cookie they wanted to speak with me and my help about you."

"Following—" Kitty's eyes looked up and down the dark street. It was disturbing to imagine that some reporter might have been following her around all day and she hadn't even been aware of it.

"Yes. I expect you to be more circumspect in the future."

"Yes, Mrs. Randall."

The woman pushed and the door half-shut.

Kitty stuck out her hand. "Wait."

"Yes?" Mrs. Randall looked at her narrowly.

"I mean, I just wanted to say how sorry I am about Rich Evan's passing."

Mrs. Randall cocked her head. "You mean that *rock person* that I heard on the news had died?"

Kitty nodded. "Yes, I'm so sorry."

A bemused eyebrow arched her way. "Why are you telling me this?"

"Well, I mean, Mr. Evan was your friend and all and I—"

Mrs. Randall managed a slight chuckle. This was about the best a woman like her could do. Tickle her feet and she'd look at you as if you'd lost your mind. "I assure you that musician was no friend of mine." Her hand was on the door.

Kitty talked quickly. "But Mr. Evan was my client. I fed his puppy, Benny. I was told that you had referred me. That's how I'd gotten the job."

"That's impossible, dear. You are mistaken."

"Are you certain?"

Mrs. Randall dropped her eyebrow. No one questioned her authority and got away with it.

Kitty backed down.

"Now, if you don't mind?" The hand gave the door a push.

Kitty couldn't let go. "But if you didn't recommend Mr. Evan, who did?"

Mrs. Randall was losing patience. "I really wouldn't know. Perhaps, it was my husband, Mr. Randall. He deals with all sorts in his business."

"Yes, I suppose so."

"Goodnight, Miss Karlyle."

Kitty nodded. Her audience was over. The door closed

quietly with a click.

# 9

It was way too late when Velma finally dropped Kitty off at her apartment.

Poor Velma had to chauffeur Kitty around to the markets again so she'd have everything she needed for the next day's meals. It was nearly eleven p.m. when Velma and Granny's Chrysler chug-chugged away in search of a bed of her own.

Climbing the building's steps, Kitty's legs might have been lead-filled. Had someone, a mad doctor with a minor in geology, replaced her leg bones with lead replicas?

Sylvester, one of the high-spirited musicians living next door, was sitting on the top step. He was a skinny twenty year old with slick black hair, a bad case of acne and big dreams of making it in L.A. Los Angeles was full of dreams. Some came true and some didn't. And kids like Sylvester never stopped coming, never stopped trying to climb the ladder. Kitty was fond of him and hoped he would one day find success.

"You look crummy." He scooted aside to let Kitty pass.

"I feel crummy." Kitty pushed her hair from her face.

"What happened to your apartment?" He stood. "You have a party earlier—one of those crazy Hollywood parties everybody always hears about?"

Was that a tad of envy she noted in his question? "A party? What do you mean?"

"I took Fred out for a walk," explained Sylvester. The guys had a key to her apartment and helped look after her dog. Sylvester was from the Midwest and had grown up with dogs around the family farm. He missed having his own pet now and often took Fred out for a walk when Kitty was out. "Your place is a wreck."

"That was the police," she said, putting her key in the lock.

"The police?"

Sylvester followed Kitty inside while she explained. Fred barked hello. Barney went immediately to his food dish. That was just like him. Food first, chat later.

"That's tough." Sylvester avoided Kitty's gaze. "To tell you the truth, me and the guys heard about Rich Evan's death on the news."

"Oh." Kitty was on the floor giving Barney his evening meal.

"Tough break. The guy was good. But we don't think you had anything to do with it," he added quickly.

Kitty rose and brushed cat hair from her hounds tooth slacks. "Thanks."

"In fact, we've got a gig tonight at the Roxy. I can get you in free if you'd like to come. You should," Sylvester said. "It will cheer you up."

"I don't know. . ."

"Come on, Kitty. We go on at one."

Kitty was shaking her head. "Thanks." She hated to disappoint the boy. She suspected he had a slight crush on her. "But I'm beat. And one is a little late for this working girl."

Kitty yawned to prove her point. "All I want is to go to sleep and forget that today, like yesterday, ever happened."

Sylvester stopped at the door. "If you change your mind—"

Kitty was leaning over the kitchen counter. Her fists held her chin. "I know, Roxy, one o'clock."

Sylvester was gone. Kitty swallowed a glass of lukewarm tapwater, locked the door and turned out the lights. Barney followed her to the bedroom. Fred was already snoring on the living room sofa.

Kitty stripped and dropped into bed. She'd shower in the morning.

It was the rattling that woke her. Kitty sat up. Barney, who'd been making himself cozy on her stomach, complained and went off in search of firmer ground. Earthquake?

Kitty held her breath and listened. She strained to hear. It had almost sounded like someone was in the kitchen. "Fred?" she whispered. Kitty pulled the bed sheet up and wrapped it around herself like an over-sized toga.

The familiar sound of Fred's claws chick-chicking over the tiles calmed her. Fred walked into the room. A faint light came through the blinds. His tail was wagging.

He pushed his face up on the mattress. She rubbed his nose. "Oh, it was only you. What's wrong? You need to go out? Are you hungry?"

Kitty glanced at the clock on her night table. She'd barely been asleep half an hour. It was two minutes till midnight. The witching hour.

She heard a creak. Fred heard it too and turned his head towards the open bedroom door. "Barney?" Kitty leaned forward, afraid to breathe. Barney wasn't answering.

Finally she jumped off the bed. "This is crazy," she said aloud. Her heart was racing. "I'm making myself crazy. Ever since poor Mr. Evan died, I've been letting everything get to me. Well," she said, leaving the bedroom, "not anymore."

Fred followed her up the narrow hall, a reassuring and sharp-toothed presence. Kitty stopped at the entryway to the living room. A chill ran up her spine and spiraled out of control to her hands and toes.

The front door was ajar.

Kitty was thinking, *I know I locked that.* She was positive. It was right after Sylvester left. So how did the front door get opened again?

Kitty reached out her hand for Fred and felt his familiar warmth. At least he's not barking, she thought. That's a good sign. She prayed. Isn't it?

It meant there were no evil, hooded strangers lurking in dark, shadow filled corners clutching long and dangerous kitchen knives. Didn't it?

Kitty's other hand felt for the light switch. It was around here someplace. Her fingers found it and after only a moment's hesitation the room was bathed in stark white light. Barney mewled. He was licking his chops beside his bowl of water under the kitchen counter.

There was no one here. Kitty took in a long-deserved breath. Going to the front door, she examined the lock. It looked okay. There was no sign of it having been broken and there was no damage to the door.

Kitty explored outside. All was quiet and all was dark, at least by L.A. standards. Still, this was all too spooky. And she remembered how Mrs. Randall had said some reporter claimed to have been following her around all day without her knowing. She shivered and ran back inside.

After calling 911 and giving her name and address, Kitty called Velma and got her answering machine. "Vel, this is Kitty. I know you're probably asleep and I'm sorry to call so late. But if you can hear me, please pick up."

Kitty listened a moment, her ear pressed to the receiver. There was no response. "Call me when you get this."

Kitty didn't let Officer Prinze into her apartment until he'd shown her two forms of ID. "Man, the perp made a mess of this place, didn't he?" Prinze took off his cap and scratched his head.

"No," said Kitty. "I mean, the place was already like this."

Prinze lifted an eyebrow.

Kitty knew exactly what he was thinking. "I don't normally keep the apartment this way." She crossed her arms. "The police made this mess when they were searching the place."

"Searching the place?" Prinze's eyes narrowed and he

seemed to stiffen.

Kitty explained.

Prinze nodded. "Right. So what makes you think you were burgled, Miss Karlyle?"

Kitty told the officer about the open door. Prinze examined the entry as Kitty retold her story. Prinze shrugged. "Everything looks good to me. Maybe you only forgot to lock it."

Kitty shook her head. "I'm positive I did. I remember clearly."

"Then maybe the door wasn't shut all the way. You could have turned the lock and the door was ajar," said Prinze. "A little gust of wind and open she went. Really, isn't that possible, miss?"

Kitty said she didn't think so.

"All I can do," Prinze explained in a tired voice, "is write it up." He did so and departed.

Kitty locked the door behind him. "That was a waste of time, wasn't it, Fred?"

Fred wagged.

"And I have locked this door." Kitty jiggled the handle and pointed her finger at the dog. "You're my witness."

Fang yawned. He was bone tired. His hands reached for his coffee mug. He tipped his brew up to his lips and drained the bitter dregs and spat. Coffee wasn't doing it. What he needed was a hit. He opened a shallow drawer beneath the console and pulled out a small bag.

In a few minutes he'd feel like he'd chugged sixteen cups of coffee. But he was paying the price.

He emptied the bag and went back to work. The two men on the sofa behind him had fallen asleep. They were money men. And he hated them. He hated them because they controlled all the money and all the drugs and all the world or so it seemed.

And he hated them because he needed them.

With renewed energy, he dove back into his work. If all went well, he wouldn't need them much longer. Fang nodded to the young girl in the vocal booth and rolled tape. She was pretty good and he'd gotten her cheap. She was cute looking but not spectacular, with thin hips and a boyish figure packaged in a pair of jeans and an oyster shell colored silk blouse.

Fang smiled as her sweet voice carried through the monitors. He kept the levels low, not wanting to waken the others. The girl's name was Mila. He glanced at his watch. He'd keep her working another hour. Then it would be too late for her to go home.

She'd spend the night. With him.

The red light on the telephone blinked and he picked it up. "Hey, baby," he purred. It was Angela. "Have you heard from the lawyers yet?"

"No," Angela said. "At least nothing useful."

"I don't understand, Angie." Fang dropped the vocal levels a smidgen. "Since you and Rich weren't legally divorced at the time of his death, everything should go to you." There was a sense of urgency in his voice that he couldn't control.

"Yes, well, tell that to the courts." She sighed. "It's all this murder stuff that's got everything else screwed up. If they'd just lock up that pet girl and be done with it, the courts might speed everything up," Angela said. "At least, that's what the lawyer tells me."

"I'm counting on this money, baby," Fang said, his voice as hard-edged as a granite slab.

"You're counting on it?" said Angela. "That money's mine. And I intend to get it."

Fang trembled. "Yes, of course." If she pulled the rug out from under him, he was sunk. He was in deep. Too deep. He had to be very careful how he handled things.

"I was just thinking how good it would be for the both of us to get all this b.s. out of the way," Fang said quickly, "so we can be together."

"And so you can get your record out?" Angela's voice sounded firm and unwilling to listen to any nonsense. "I'm not a fool, Fang, darling, and don't you forget it."

Fang held his breath. "Of course, baby." He apologized. "It's late and I'm a little nuts. I've got Frick and Frack here breathing down my neck." He squeezed the receiver in his hand and whispered, "This record is important to me, Angie."

"Don't worry," Angela said. "When the sharks are circling, what do you do?"

He sighed and rubbed his cheek. "I don't know. I'm tired. It's too late for games."

"Feed them."

Angela hung up. Fang looked at the phone with distaste. It was just as well she'd ended the conversation, Mila had finished her track and entered the control room.

"How was I?" she asked meekly.

Fang pushed back his chair and took her hand. "Lovely."

"Thanks. I can do it again, if you like. I thought maybe I was weak on the bridge."

Fang shook his head. "No, you were perfect." In truth he'd barely been listening since he'd been on the phone with Angela. "Besides, it's late." He rubbed her neck. "I'll bet you're beat."

"Yeah," she said, "I guess I am." Mila picked her purse up from the floor and strung it over her shoulder. "I suppose I should be going."

"It's a long drive back to Cerritos." Fang lifted her purse by its strap and laid it down on the warm console. "Maybe you should spend the night?"

Mila looked from her purse to the two sleeping men. "Are you sure it won't be any trouble?"

"No trouble at all," he answered smoothly. "I tell you what—why don't you go run yourself a nice warm bath? Do you a world of good. You can use my tub."

"I don't know. . ." She glanced at the sleeping men.

Fang opened the door to the hall. Benny was sleeping beside it. "End of the hall. I'll come check on you as soon as I've cleaned up and said goodnight to our guests." His smile was ten thousand watts of Marquis de Sade seduction hidden behind a carefully contrived mask of Ward Cleaver concern.

Mila nodded and padded away barefooted. She'd left her sandals in the control room. She wouldn't be needing them tonight. Fang laid them next to her purse and turned off the gear. She wouldn't be needing anything tonight. Nothing besides the love he was going to give her.

Fang roused his two guests and saw them out. Before they left, he said, "I'm going to need another bag."

"It's going to cost you," replied the taller of the two men. "Same as always."

"Add it to my bill." Fang said sourly. "I'm good for it."

The tall man nodded, grabbed his half-awake friend by the elbow and led him out to their car.

"Good riddance," muttered Fang. He turned his eyes to the ceiling. He hoped Mila was still in the tub. It was large enough for two.

# 10

It had been three days since Rich Evan had died and Kitty was still feeling like she was living under a giant microscope.

She was also pretty sure that somebody was tailing her. It seemed like the whole world was watching her with big accusing eyes that said, 'We know what you did.' It was making her edgy.

Her dark mood was a sharp and unwelcome contrast to the cheery Southern California sky. And Kitty was determined to do something about it. Maybe she should get a new hair style? Or a new hair color? Blue, maybe.

At least there had not been any further incidents at her apartment. And Kitty had become obsessive-compulsive about shutting and locking all the doors and windows whether she was staying home or going out.

Kitty had instructed the guys next door to be the same

when they used her place, but she needn't have bothered as they'd lost her spare key. She'd have to remember to have a new one made. It was just like those guys. Sweet but careless.

Det. Young's house was a bunker-looking white rectangle on a sidestreet from which Kitty could hear the hiss of traffic on nearby Victory Boulevard. The grass was brown and patchy. A chain link fence protected the backyard; from what she couldn't imagine.

Kitty pulled into the drive behind a late model, red Jeep Wrangler.

A black Lab answered the door, pushing her snout against the screen to get a better noseful of the new arrival.

Well, thought Kitty, at least he does have a Lab, like he said. She rapped on the aluminum screendoor. The dog barked.

"Okay, okay! I'm coming." The detective's voice was muffled and distant. "It's you." His surprise was evident on his face.

It was the first time that Kitty had really noticed the young detective as a person, not a cop. His eyes were pale green, the color of steamed, julienned green beans and he had fine brown hair. Kitty figured he'd look even more handsome if he'd let his hair grow out some instead of keeping it in that harsh, unflattering crewcut that made his head look way too square.

Young dropped a trowel onto the side table near his sofa and unlatched the door. "Come on in." His hands were covered with black soil and he wiped them on his shorts.

The Lab shot past him and jumped up on Kitty, placing her paws on Kitty's chest. Kitty fell off the porch backwards and landed on the sidewalk.

"Lib!" remonstrated Young. He ran to Kitty's rescue. He lifted her and wagged his finger at the dog. "I am so sorry about that." He turned to the dog. "Bad girl. Bad."

The dog hung her head and sulked.

"It's okay." Kitty managed a smile. "Nothing's broken or torn." She clapped her hands and the dog came right to her. "Libby, right?"

Young nodded.

"That's a good girl, Libby. I know you didn't mean to push. You don't know your own strength, that's all."

Libby gave Kitty a couple of licks. "I should have brought you something to eat," began Kitty, "that's what I should have done."

"That isn't necessary. Believe me," said Young, "Libby eats just fine."

Kitty rose. "I remember. Out of a can."

"That's right," Young said defensively. " See how healthy she looks?"

"Looks can be deceiving," Kitty replied pointedly.

"Besides, sometimes I bring her home an Arby's." Young grinned.

Kitty rolled her eyes. "You poor thing," she said to Libby. Libby barked.

"Come on inside and get cleaned up if you like." The detective held open the screendoor.

Kitty paced the small front room. "Very nice." There was a rickety yellow sofa with one front leg about a half-inch shorter than the other, two small end tables and a diploma from the L.A. Sheriff's Academy in a cheap, smudgy frame on the wall above the sofa. Not exactly Better Homes and Gardens, but her folks had raised her to be polite.

"Yeah, right." Young let Libby out in the backyard through the kitchen and returned to the living room. "Have a seat." He motioned to the sofa. "I was working in the yard."

"You're a gardener?" It seemed so out of character. He was a cop after all. She would have figured his hobby would be lifting weights, going to the shooting range or maybe sharpening his exotic weaponry collection. Kitty sat on the edge of the sofa and the flimsy cushion curled up around her legs like a Venus Flytrap.

"I like to mess around." He rubbed his dirty hands together. "Helps me relax."

Kitty nodded. "I'm sure police work is very stressful."

For the first time since her arrival, Young smiled. "Yeah, well, if I had to go around cooking for the pampered cats and dogs of the upper class like you do everyday—" He left his thought unfinished.

"I don't think of it that way."

"How do you think of it?"

"I think of it as getting the opportunity to practice my skills on customers who truly love my cooking. And you know what else?" she asked.

"No. What?"

Kitty grinned. "If my customers don't like what I feed them, or it's undercooked or cold, too salty, not salty enough—"

The detective raised an eyebrow.

"—they can't complain."

Young tipped back his head and laughed. It was a deep, wholly natural laugh that bared his teeth and brought tiny wrinkle lines to the corners of his eyes and made her want to smile too.

Young said, "Can I get you something to drink?"

"What have you got?"

He shrugged. "Soda, water."

"Soda water?"

"Sure." He returned with two bottles of cold lemon-flavored Perrier. "So," he said as he dropped down on the opposite end of the sofa, "how did you find me and what do you want?"

"I found you by going to the LASD. Malibu substation. A nice man there gave me your address. He even wrote out directions." Kitty pulled a crumpled sheet of paper from her purse and showed it to Young.

"Nice. I'm gonna have to thank him. You remember his name?"

Kitty thought a moment. "No, sorry. As for why I'm here, I wanted to find out what's happening with Mr. Evan's death."

"You mean his murder."

Kitty bit her lip. "Is it really so certain?"

"It's certain alright. This town's got a lot of drugs floating around, anybody can get them. But Barbados nut doesn't just fall from the sky, even in L.A." He paused dramatically. His green eyes pierced her defenses. "And you're our main suspect."

She squirmed. The way he'd said 'you're our main suspect' made her feel like she was about to become his main course. "But I didn't do anything."

"I'm not saying you're guilty," Young said, "but I've got to tell you, there are a lot of folks in the department and in the D.A.'s office who think otherwise."

"Is that why the police have been following me around?"

He leaned towards Kitty. "What do you mean? As far as I know, nobody's following you anywhere."

"Oh."

"Are you sure you're being followed? This could be important."

"Well, no," confessed Kitty. "I just feel like I'm being watched."

"That's normal," he said with a shrug. "You're feeling guilty whether you are or not. It's a natural reaction, like cringing when a police car is in the traffic lane behind you. Everybody gets that way. Sometimes I forget I'm a cop and react that way myself."

Kitty was nodding. "I suppose. But then there was that break-in the other night."

Once again the detective expressed his surprise and Kitty explained how she was certain her door had been opened while she slept.

"That's news to me. But like the LAPD told you, it could have been nothing."

Young rose and took a long sip of his mineral water. "Listen, Miss Karlyle, I still don't think you're coming clean with me." His eyes barreled in on her. "What is it you really want? You didn't drive all the way out to Burbank for a glass of water."

Kitty swallowed and squeezed the Perrier bottle between

her legs. "I want to know who killed Mr. Evan." She stood now. "And I want whoever is following me to stop. And I want the press to leave me alone."

Her voice was rising. "I just want to be able to do my job without worrying about the police and murderers and everybody thinking that I had anything to do with any of this!"

Young applauded lightly. "Nice speech."

She scowled and marched to the door. "Thanks for your sympathy. I should have known better."

The detective stopped Kitty with a hand on her arm. "I want the same thing you do—Rich Evan's killer. It's my job to find him," he looked in her eyes, "or her."

"I did not kill Rich Evan," Kitty said through clenched teeth.

"Then who did?"

Kitty pulled her arm free. "I don't know." She pushed out the door. "But I'm going to find out."

"Leave it alone, Miss Karlyle. That's a job for the police."

She threw open her car door and climbed inside. Her phone was ringing. She reached into her purse and pushed the button. "Yes?" she barked.

"Are you sure?" Kitty paled. "Is he okay?" Kitty nodded. "I'll be right there, Mr. Randall. Give me the address."

Det. Young approached the car. "What's that? Is something wrong?"

"That was Mr. Randall, one of my clients. Mr. Cookie is in the hospital."

"Mr. Cookie?"

Kitty's pupils grew large and round and her voice

92

trembled. "They think he was poisoned."

# 11

They took Det. Young's Jeep to the Landau Veterinary Clinique and Spa of Beverly Hills where a valet, much to Young's annoyance, insisted on parking his car. Reluctantly, the detective pushed a crumpled dollar bill in the kid's hand. "There better not be any scratches on it when I get back!"

Kitty couldn't help feeling sorry for the valet. There were already twenty-odd scratches that she could count and that was just along the front fender on her side of the Jeep. Looked like Libby had used the car for a scratching post. What was the valet supposed to do? Buff them all out?

Young hopped out and ran to catch up with Kitty who was already at the entrance where another well-dressed young man was holding the door for her. "Can you believe this?" grumbled Young. "A doorman and a valet—at a vet's office, for crying out loud. And I am not tipping him." The detective jerked his head in the direction of the doorman.

Kitty ignored Young's grumblings and raced to the reception desk where a platinum blonde who looked like she ought to be out auditioning for a role as the next Bond Girl was buffing her nails. "I'm Kitty Karlyle," she said breathlessly. "I'm here to see Mr. Cookie. Is he all right?"

Blondie looked up. "The doctor is with him now. Examination Room Three." She pointed up the hall with her nail file.

Kitty, with Det. Young in her wake, walked quickly up the corridor. Her footsteps echoed loudly on the black granite floor. The door to the examination room was open. She marveled. The large examining room looked like it had been done up by an interior decorator with a budget larger than Kitty's next year's projected income.

Mr. Cookie lay on his side. Mr. Randall was conferring with an elegant looking African-American in gray slacks and a white smock; no doubt the doctor.

Mrs. Randall was stroking Mr. Cookie and looked up as Kitty and the detective came bursting in. Mr. Cookie barely managed to raise his head. His tail didn't stir.

Kitty stopped in her tracks and Det. Young bumped into her from behind. He whistled softly, his eyes drawn to a wall-mounted 42" plasma screen TV displaying an idyllic forest scene. The picture was so clear and realistic, he could almost smell the pine needles.

"Is he okay?" Kitty asked softly.

"Yes," said Mrs. Randall, quietly, her hand never stopping. Back and forth, back and forth, she stroked the little guy. "Dr. Landau says Mr. Cookie appears to be out of danger now."

Dr. Landau and the three-piece suited Mr. Randall stopped their conversation and the doctor turned his attention to Kitty. "Are you the one that feeds Mr. Cookie?"

Kitty nodded. Why did it suddenly feel like the walls were closing in on her? Why did she suddenly feel like this outwardly serene looking veterinary clinic had turned into a Temple of Doom?

"Mind telling me just what you gave him this morning?" The doctor's hand fell onto a file. Mr. Cookie's file no doubt.

"Here We Go Round the Mahi Go Round."

"What?" Dr. Landau shot a look at Mr. Randall who merely shrugged his soft, round shoulders.

"Here We Go Round the Mahi Go Round." Kitty turned to Det. Young for support but he'd chosen this particular moment to look at his feet. "It's Mahi Mahi," she said quickly, "with mixed vegetables and couscous."

The doctor said, "And some heavy duty laxative, I'd say. Had to be to cause that strong a case of diarrhea."

"You should see my car," spoke Mr. Randall.

"The Rolls," sniffed Mrs. Randall, "is a mess."

Dr. Landau was shaking his head. "We'll get the results of the blood tests in the morning," he said to Mrs. Randall. "I'm sure Mr. Cookie is going to pull through, but you had better watch his diet," he added, "*carefully.*"

"But there couldn't have been anything in my dish to have caused Mr. Cookie to be sick," said Kitty. "I prepare everything myself. Maybe someone else in the household fed him something?"

"Impossible," stated Mrs. Randall. "This is forbidden."

Kitty addressed Dr. Landau. "Couldn't he maybe have an allergy to Mahi Mahi or one of the other ingredients? Couldn't that have made him sick?"

Det. Young cleared his throat. "Excuse me, doc," he interrupted, "but you said diarrhea?"

"That's correct."

"I'd like to see a copy of those reports when you get them. If you don't mind."

"Who are you?" Mrs. Randall's tiny eyes finally seemed to notice the poorly dressed stranger.

"Det. Jack Young, Los Angeles Sheriff's Department." He held out a hand. Since it was dirty, Mrs. Randall merely glanced at it dismissively.

Mr. Randall skirted around the stainless steel examination table, however, and shook the detective's hand. "What's your interest in this, young man?" Mr. Randall looked meaningfully at Kitty. "Are you two an item as they say?"

Kitty blushed.

"No, sir," Det. Young replied with a grin. "I'm investigating Rich Evan's murder. He was poisoned by something called the Barbados nut. I'd like to find out if your Mr. Cookie here ingested the same thing."

"Barbados nut," Dr. Landau said thoughtfully. "Yes," he said, tapping his jaw with a long, finely manicured finger, "that would do it all right."

Outside Dr. Landau's office, Young tapped his foot while waiting impatiently for the kid to bring his car around. He looked at his watch. "How long can it take to get valet service at a freaking veterinary clinic?" he complained.

Kitty ignored his complaints. She had bigger problems. Far bigger problems. Rich Evan was dead. Mr. Cookie might have been killed. What was going on? Was she somehow responsible or was this only some awful coincidence?

Was she dishing up death? She'd have to close down her business. Stop cooking altogether. She wouldn't go anywhere near food for fear she'd poison someone else. Maybe she should ask Dr. Landau about the possibility of interning with him as a veterinary assistant.

No, Kitty shook her head. After what happened to Mr. Cookie and the way Dr. Landau and the Randalls were all looking at her—like she was Lizzie Borden's sister and Lizzie was the good sister—he'd never hire her. Not even to clean out the cages. And she couldn't blame him.

"Hey," Young shook her. "Wake up, the car's here. You coming?"

Kitty's lower lip trembled. Her eyes turned glassy.

"Oh, no," Young said, "don't—"

Kitty began to sob.

"—cry," sighed the detective. He opened the passenger door and helped Kitty up.

They stopped at a Starbucks on Sunset Boulevard for coffee and, though he tried to draw her out, Kitty barely spoke.

Young dropped some bills on the table and they drove back to his place in silence. "I've got to go on duty in an hour." He opened Kitty's car door and she quietly slipped behind the wheel of her Volvo. "But don't worry. We'll get to the bottom of this. Rich Evan's murderer is out there somewhere." He rapped the car door with his knuckles. "I'll find him."

Kitty cocked her head. "I thought you believed I was a murderer, that I killed Mr. Evan?" She rubbed her eyes. They were red and itchy from crying. It was embarrassing to cry in front of a stranger, a policeman no less, but she hadn't been able to help herself and was all the more infuriated because of this lack of self control.

"Nah," Young drawled, "you may be a lousy cook, but I don't think you're a killer."

"Excuse me? A lousy—"

"Sorry, I mean chef."

Kitty flared, fire coming back to life inside her gut. "I am not a lousy cook."

"I don't know about that." His eyes danced. Was there a hint of mischief in them? "Rich Evan and Mr. Cookie might disagree with you there."

He was grinning, big and toothy, and Kitty felt like socking him, knocking a few of those white teeth loose for him. So smug, so full of himself. "So why," Kitty demanded angrily, "are you helping me, detective?"

"I'm helping myself," Young said as he headed up the walk to his door. "Catching killers is part of my job." He stopped at the door and crossed his arms, holding the screendoor open with his foot. "Besides, I've got to prove you're innocent."

"You do, do you?" What was it with this guy? Did he get a kick out of watching other people's blood boil?

Kitty stuck her head out the window and yelled. "And just why do you have to do that?" With one hand, she thrust the key into the ignition like she was skewering a small bird and twisted.

"Because it wouldn't look good for me, being on the force as I happen to be, if you were a convicted murderess."

"What?" Kitty hissed through her teeth.

"Seeing as how I'm going to marry you." He beamed and went inside. The screendoor banged shut.

Kitty hollered, "Excuse me?" Her foot pressed down on the accelerator and only stopped when the pedal hit the floorboard. The engine hollered.

Det. Young reappeared, his nose pressed against the inside of the screen. "Hey, you keep saying Libby ought to eat healthier. What better way than you marrying me? Lib will be your responsibility then. You want her to eat better? Feed her better."

Kitty clung to the wheel, listening in stunned, seething silence. Why didn't he shut up already?

"I can't afford to hire you, so I've decided to marry you." Young looked at his watch. "Well," he said with a waist-high wave, "got to go." With that, the solid wood door swung closed.

"EXCUSE ME?!" Kitty's eyes bugged out of her head. The engine was howling and she took her foot off the gas. A man out mowing his front lawn stared at her. She made a face and thrust out her tongue. The man looked away.

Kitty stuck her head back inside the car. "Why, that arrogant, conceited, tasteless, tactless," her hands pounded the dash until it cracked, "obnoxious man."

Kitty was spitting mad and she pulled down the drive with a squeal of rubber. Det. Young had a lot of nerve. "Marry her! She'd rather die first. She'd rather marry Fang

Danson first!

And she ought to report Det. Jack Young to the ASPCA for the way he treated that poor dog of his.

That's what she ought to do.

# 12

Perhaps to prove her point, Kitty drove until she found herself at Fang Danson's home. It was Fang's personal assistant, Derrick, a pasty-faced, dark-haired young man with an acne scarred face, who let her inside and led her into the den.

Fang, stretched out on a black leather sofa, turned his head away from the college football game he'd been engrossed in. "Time to feed the doggie, is it?"

"Actually, no."

Fang sat up. He grabbed the remote and turned down the volume. "What is it then?"

"I wanted to talk to you—about the other day."

Fang leered. "Get us some drinks, Derrick. What will you have?"

Kitty looked from one man to the other. "It doesn't

matter. I'll have whatever you're having."

Fang nodded. "Two Stellas." He motioned for Kitty to join him on the sofa. "You follow American football?"

"Not really."

Fang turned off the set.

Derrick returned shortly with two tall glasses of beer. Kitty wasn't much of a drinker but she took a sip, caught mostly foam and coughed.

"Where's Benny?"

"Out back, I expect," replied Fang. "The little guy likes to sleep in the shade." He sidled closer. "So what is it precisely about the other day that you would like to discuss, Kit?" His voice sounded oily and hot as an over-cooked french fry.

Kitty held her glass close to her chest, a liquid barrier between herself and Fang Danson. "I haven't seen you the last several times that I've come to feed Benny. It's almost as if you've been avoiding me," she gulped, "Fang." Kitty nearly choked on her words.

Kitty had trouble calling him by his first name, but knew he would like it. As for Fang having been avoiding her, she liked that. "I don't want there to be any hard feelings."

"Fang Danson doesn't have time for hard feelings." He leered and swigged his beer. "At least not *that* kind of hard feelings, if you know what I mean?"

He fluttered his eyelashes and set down his glass. "I'm not much of a ladies man, you know, Kit." His arm snaked out along the back of the couch, making its snake-like way towards her shoulders. "Not like Rich was."

Kitty leaned forward.

"It's just that there's something special about you."

"What do you mean 'not like Rich was'?"

Fang shrugged. "Rich was into the ladies. Nothing wrong with that. Famous ladies, single ladies, married ladies." His hand had fallen on Kitty's knee. "Fat ladies, skinny ladies. It didn't matter none to Rich."

"I see." Kitty inched away but she'd hit the side of the sofa and had no room left to maneuver. "Tell me, when was the last time you saw Mr. Evan?"

Fang sat back. "That was the night before he was found dead at his house. We'd hung out at a club together."

"What club was that?"

"The Disco Den. Ever hear of it?"

"No, I haven't."

"Nice place, up on Sunset. I could take you there sometime, if you like."

"Sure," said Kitty, uneasily, "that would be nice." She plucked his hand from her knee. "So that was the last time you spoke to Mr. Evan. Did he seem normal to you?"

Fang laughed. "There wasn't nothing normal about Rich Evan. He was an artist. Artists," he said, tapping his skull, "aren't normal."

Amen to that, thought Kitty. "And everything seemed ordinary? I mean, he didn't behave differently and you didn't notice anything unusual?"

"Nope. We left the club. I had to get back because I had some sessions booked here for the next morning. Rich, he wanted to keep going. Find some action."

"Action?"

"Yeah, find a bird. Know what I mean?"

"I think I do." And she found it disgusting. "Do you

know who she was?" This mystery woman could be important.

"No." Fang scratched his neck. "I don't remember Rich saying."

"Oh." Kitty sounded deflated. There were millions of women in Southern California. Unless the woman came forward, she'd be nearly impossible to find.

"And that wasn't the last time that I talked to him."

"It wasn't?" Kitty leaned towards Fang. "You talked to him again?"

Fang nodded.

"When?"

"He called me in the morning." Fang chuckled. "Said he'd gotten lucky. Ah, well, at least he had some fun before he died. Good for him."

"Got lucky? You mean with a girl?"

"I don't mean playing poker." Fang drained his glass. "You're hardly drinking. Finish up, I'll get you another."

Kitty rose. "No, I really should be going. I have so much cooking to do."

Fang came to his feet and laid his hand lightly on her shoulder. "About that. The cooking. Since you're cooking for Benny, what do you say you cook for me, too?"

"Cook for you?" This caught Kitty by surprise.

"Sure, I'll pay you. The stuff you're cooking up smells terrific. I wouldn't mind getting some myself."

"What about Derrick?"

Fang waved his hand. "He's a gofer, nothing more. Of course, he calls himself a personal assistant. What a load that is. Everybody's got to have himself a title these days. And then there's the woman who cleans the house."

His lip curled. "What's her name? Doesn't matter," he shrugged, "wouldn't trust her to cook toast. She barely cleans." He smiled broadly. "How's about it, Kit?"

Once again she cringed. She hated it when he called her Kit. "Well," said Kitty, "I don't know. I never really gave much thought to cooking for people, too." It would be a lot more work. Then again, it would mean a lot more money. The corner of her lip turned down. And possibly a lot more problems. Complaints.

"I don't know," she said, not wanting to anger him. "I'll have to think about it."

"You do that," said Fang amicably, following her out the door.

She unlocked her car. "So I suppose you were home the morning Mr. Evan died?"

"That's right," he said casually. "And all that night, too. I came home. I went to bed."

"Alone?"

He tucked his chin into his chest. "That's right. Sleeping. Alone. I told you, I'm a one woman man."

She started the engine and rolled down her window. "You don't suppose it could have been his ex-wife, do you?"

"I don't suppose who could have been his ex-wife?" Fang looked perplexed.

"The woman Mr. Evan slept with. Do you think it could have been his ex-wife?"

Fang grinned. "Which one? Pamela, Tracy," he ticked the names off on his fingers, "Chloe. . ?"

Kitty blanched. "How many ex-wives did Mr. Evan

have?"

"Three—four, if you count Angela."

"I don't understand. Consuelo told me Rich Evan and Angela were divorced. Do you mean they weren't?"

"Not yet. Not officially, depending on how you're counting."

"So maybe he'd slept with Angela before he died? She could have a motive."

A dark cloud passed over Fang's face. His pupils narrowed. "Angela? A motive for what?"

"For killing Mr. Evan."

Fang clenched his hands. "That's impossible," he said. "Angela wouldn't hurt a fly. Besides, I don't care what the police say. Rich Evan lived hard and died hard. And his ticker wasn't what it should be."

"You mean his heart."

"That's right. He'd seen a specialist in Beverly Hills about it. Had himself some sort of murmur. The doc told him to take better care of himself." Fang shook his head. "But Rich didn't believe in doing anything halfway. He lived life to the fullest," Fang paused, "to the end."

"Maybe. But the police are sure that he was murdered."

Fang shrugged. "The police have been wrong before. They'll no doubt be wrong again." He leaned over the Volvo. "If you want to know the truth, it was that house that killed him."

Kitty's brow shot up. "The house?"

"That's right. The place is haunted. Cursed!" He banged the roof of the car so hard that she jumped out of her seat. "But you don't hear the cops talking about that now, do you?" He shook his head. "No, you don't."

Kitty didn't know what to think. Fang sounded scared and almost bitter. "I still don't understand—"

Fang lowered his voice and said in a frightening manner. "You don't know the history of that house, do you?"

She shook her head slowly.

"Well," he began, "let me tell you. That house is haunted. There's been a curse on it for more than sixty years." He held up his fingers. "I told Rich not to move into that place. I'd heard the stories. But he wouldn't listen. Rich never listened to anybody. And now he's dead.

"Four people have died in that house. Five if you count poor Rich now. Two movie stars, a film director and a lawyer." He paused and took a shallow breath. "Now Rich."

Fang's warm breath rushed across her face. She tasted fear. She looked skeptical.

"Don't believe in ghosts, do you?"

"Well. . ."

"How about evil? Do you believe in evil, Kit?"

With a tremble, she managed to nod.

"Well," Fang's thin white-knuckled hands gripped the edge of the car door, "that house is evil. It kills everybody."

# 13

Kitty pulled into Rich Evan's driveway.

Consuelo's car was up in front of the garage. Was the place really haunted? she wondered. Or was Fang only trying to scare her, playing a prank on her? If so, why?

Was he hoping she'd stay away from the house? Was the clue to Rich Evan's death inside and was Fang Danson a part of it in some way? What had he been doing in Rich's den the other day when she'd burst in on him? Was he looking for something?

Well, thought Kitty, I'm going to find out. Even if it kills me, she mused; then quickly took back her thoughts.

As she headed up the drive, she heard a sob and turned. A chubby woman in high-back khaki overalls was on her knees in the side garden next door. Uncombed locks of black hair fell from beneath an olive-green cartwheel hat perched on her head. Her hands held a pair of long-bladed gardening shears. Tan chukkas protected her feet.

The woman was pruning and weeding the flower beds. A small pile of shriveled weeds lay in a clump beside a small trowel.

"Hi," said Kitty.

The woman gave a start. "Oh!"

"Is everything all right?"

The woman raised a gloved hand to her nose and sniffed. "Yes, fine." She laid down her shears. "Are you the realtor or the new buyer, perhaps?" The woman rose and dusted off her knees.

"No." Kitty held out her hand. "I'm Kitty Karlyle. I worked for Mr. Evan."

The woman's eyes teared up and the drops began to fall. "Oh, dear," she said, "I am sorry. It's just so hard to imagine poor Rich, I mean, Mr. Evan, being-being gone." Her chest heaved.

Kitty wrapped her arms around the woman's shoulders. "There now," she said. "Everything's all right now."

The woman nodded. "I'm so sorry. I don't know what's come over me. I'm Florence Goodman. My husband, Stephen and I were Mr. Evan's neighbors."

"You and Mr. Evan must have been close." Did she smell alcohol on the woman's breath?

Mrs. Goodman stared at the lawn. "He was a very nice man."

"Yes, he was," agreed Kitty. "Did you see him the morning he died?"

"No!" Mrs. Goodman, said quickly. She glanced at her

110

house. "I certainly did not!"

"I didn't mean anything—I only wondered if you'd seen or heard anything. . ."

Mrs. Goodman's back stiffened. "The police have already questioned me," she sniffed, "*and* my husband," she added. "I've nothing more to say." She turned on her heels and waddled off across the lawn and disappeared behind her front door.

Kitty stared in stunned silence. "What was that all about?" she muttered finally.

"You better hope the doctor doesn't get wind of you bothering his wife."

Kitty spun. It was Consuelo standing at the side door. "The doctor? Whatever do you mean?"

"Mr. Goodman. He doesn't like people talking to his wife."

Kitty slowly walked to the house and followed Consuelo inside. "What do you mean he doesn't like people talking to his wife? What's wrong with that?"

Consuelo swirled a finger round and round her ear. "The doctor he is loco. You know?"

Kitty nodded. Consuelo was, in her opinion, weighted on the loco side herself.

"And after what happened with Mr. Evan and Mrs. Goodman. . ." Consuelo wiped her hands on her apron and pulled open the refrigerator.

"What?" demanded Kitty. "You can't make a statement like that and simply stop." She followed Consuelo to the refrigerator. "What happened between Mr. Evan and Florence Goodman?"

The housekeeper looked incredulous. "You do not know?"

"I already said I don't know. How could I know?" She had laid her hand on Consuelo's wrist and pulled it away when the housekeeper made a face. "What don't I know?"

Consuelo smiled wickedly. In her hands she held an open bottle of champagne—a Roederer Cristal no less, worth several hundreds of dollars.

Consuelo pulled down a glass from the cabinet overhead and poured herself a generous glassful. She sat at the table—the same table where Rich Evan had eaten his last meal—sipped slowly and finally spoke. "The señor and Mrs. Goodman had some hanky-panky together." She twisted the middle and index fingers of her left hand together.

"No!" said Kitty, incredulously.

She nodded and smiled broadly. "I caught them myself. In the señor's bed. Not one week ago."

Consuelo wriggled her eyebrows. "And it wasn't the first time they had relations, if you ask me. No," she shook her head, "not at all."

Rich Evan and Florence Goodman? *Mrs.* Florence Goodman? The *dowdy* Mrs. Florence Goodman? Having an affair?

As if reading Kitty's mind and doubts, Consuelo nodded. "It's true." She refilled her glass. "The doctor, he found out. I do not know how."

Consuelo leaned forward. "He came to the house. The doctor was furious. Shouting louder than the waves. So furious he threatened to kill Mr. Evan!"

"Consuelo! Did you tell this to the police?"

The housekeeper shrugged. "No. For what? They do not ask and I do not tell."

"But Mr. Goodman could be the killer."

"They say *you* are the killer." Consuelo was looking at her quite slyly now. The housekeeper's words were slurred. "Maybe, perhaps I should not be in the same room as you? Maybe you want to kill me, too?"

Her eyes grew hard as stones. "I'm good with a knife, though." Consuelo's eyes darted to the counter and the wooden slab containing the kitchen knives. "Very, very good."

Kitty found herself inching towards the door. Her only thoughts were of escape.

"Stay," said Consuelo. "Have a glass."

"No, thank you," said Kitty, fighting to control her tremors. "I really should be going."

"Sit!" ordered the housekeeper.

Without quite knowing why, Kitty obeyed.

Consuelo smiled. "That's better." She leaned forward, her elbows on the table. "Let me tell you a story."

# 14

"I came to this country ten years ago." She held up her hands and wiggled her fingers. "I come from Guanajato. That is in Mexico."

Kitty nodded.

Consuelo wiped her lips with the inside of her arm. "I wanted to come to work for Jack Benny. My father was a huge, giant Jack Benny fan," she said wistfully. "We watched all his movies and his TV shows."

"My father, he always said, 'Go to work for Mr. Jack Benny, Consuelo. He's a great man. A funny man.'" She hung her head. "But Mr. Benny was dead."

Kitty nodded once more. She was pretty sure Jack Benny had been dead long before Consuelo had arrived in the States. "So what did you do?"

"I was forced to take temporary jobs. Cleaning jobs.

Cooking jobs. Whatever I could get. I had to send money home for my family. My father he has a clubbed foot and my younger brother is blind."

"Oh, dear," commiserated Kitty, "I am sorry."

"It happened when he was twelve. He was working after school in a fireworks factory. There was an explosion." At this moment, Consuelo's fist exploded on the kitchen table, lifting its legs right off the floor.

Kitty nearly jumped out of her skin.

"Mr. Evan he promised he would help bring Ricardo and my father to America. He promised." The housekeeper's eyes bored into Kitty's.

"How-how long have you been with Mr. Evan?"

"Six years," she spat. "Six long years." She pushed her glass aside and drank from the bottle. "All the time he keeps telling me he is going to help." The bottle slammed down on the tabletop. "But he never did." Consuelo's eyes narrowed. "And now he is muerto."

Yes, thought Kitty. So he is. And it would be so easy for Consuelo to have murdered him. Who better? She had access. After all, she lived in. That gave her plenty of opportunity. She could easily have doctored Benny's food.

But had Consuelo been trying to kill the dog to spite her boss or had she been out to get Mr. Evan himself somehow expecting that he'd eat Benny's food? Perhaps she'd even suggested that he eat it? And where had Benny been throughout all this anyway?

"I remember how shocked you looked when you came into the kitchen here and saw poor Mr. Evan lying there."

Consuelo nodded gloomily. She looked suddenly tired

and frail.

"Where was it you said you had been?"

Consuelo frowned. "I was shopping."

"Did Mr. Evan have any other visitors that morning?" Kitty asked. "Any late night guests, like Mrs. Goodman?"

Consuelo's shoulders heaved. "I do not know. Mr. Evan was not home when I went to sleep and he was not home, at least I did not see him, in the morning before I went to the market."

Kitty nodded thoughtfully. "What time did you leave for the market?"

"Why so nosy?" Consuelo barked, yet she answered anyway. "I left around nine, I think, and got back when you saw me."

So either Rich Evan had stayed out all night and returned in the late morning or he'd come in late that night and sequestered himself away with a woman. "Was his car here when you left that morning?"

Consuelo thought a moment. "No, it was not."

Kitty smiled. Now she was getting someplace.

"And I remember something else about that night."

"What?"

"The doctor and his wife had a loud argument out on the beach that evening. He was shaking her. She fell down trying to break loose."

"Then what happened?"

"She stormed out, took off in her car."

Well, well, thought Kitty, Mr. Evan's housekeeper was a bit of a snoop, wasn't she? Rich Evan and Florence Goodman could have met up for a late night rendezvous somewhere.

"Tell me, Consuelo—you mentioned telling me a story a while ago—have you ever heard any stories?" Consuelo looked puzzled. "About the house, I mean."

The housekeeper glanced nervously over her shoulder. Was she expecting a demon or an evil spirit to pounce on her? She made the sign of the cross. "It is unwise to speak of such things."

"So, you have heard the stories?"

Consuelo shook her head. "I warn you, do not talk about this house." She rose and roughly pushed back her chair. It skidded across the floor and fell over on its back.

"But, Consuelo, I only want to know—"

Consuelo cried out and ran from the room. "Uh-uh," she shouted, "do not speak about the house. The house does not like it!"

A door slammed and Kitty was all alone.

"It was over you know."

A cry escaped Kitty's lips. She turned her head. Mrs. Goodman was standing in the kitchen doorway.

Kitty said accusingly, "Mrs. Goodman, you were eavesdropping."

Mrs. Goodman shrugged. She'd removed her gloves and hat. Her hair was now neatly combed and her makeup looked freshly applied. "Only near the end. The door was ajar. Do you want to hear about it or no?"

Kitty nodded and picked up Consuelo's fallen chair. Mrs. Goodman sat. "We did have an affair," she began slowly. "Rich was a very charming man and my husband, well. . ." Her voice trailed off. "He's a cardiac surgeon. He has a very busy practice."

Kitty said she understood. It was that be polite habit thing working again. "You said it was over?"

"That's right." Mrs. Goodman was looking at her hands. "We had been seeing each other for about a month when my husband found out."

"Caught you."

Mrs. Goodman nodded. "Yes, caught us. He was so angry. You wouldn't believe it."

"Angry enough to kill?"

"Oh, no, Stephen wouldn't do that," Mrs. Goodman said quickly. "He's not the type."

Kitty wasn't so sure about that. If what Consuelo had told her she'd seen was correct, Stephen Goodman could be a violent man indeed. And he had reportedly threatened Rich Evan already. Maybe he'd finally done the deed. Yes. A doctor would certainly know all about poisons, wouldn't he?

Kitty didn't know about ghosts, but there sure was a lot of bad karma floating around this place. "Tell me, Mrs. Goodman, what do you know about the history of this house?"

For the first time, Mrs. Goodman managed a smile. "You're talking about the legends, aren't you, young lady?"

Kitty said yes.

Mrs. Goodman sighed. "Everybody wants to hear about the ghosts." She pursed her lips. Her fingers worked over the table like it was a piano. "Where shall I begin?"

"Someone told me that there had been several previous murders in this house."

"That's right. Have you ever heard of Becky Wright?"

"No. Who was she?"

"Becky Wright was a silent film actress. She'd been quite a star in her day." Mrs. Goodman leaned forward, as if the walls might hear her speak. "She was the first to die in this house."

"I see."

"What do you know about the history of Malibu, Miss Karlyle?"

"Nothing, I guess. What's there to know?"

Mrs. Goodman smiled. "This entire region of Malibu belonged to one family, the Rindge's—made their money in oil and energy, I believe."

Mrs. Goodman settled back into her chair. "In any case, they owned this whole area, including the beach. The widow allowed some folks like Barbara Stanwyck and Ronald Colman to build beach homes here in the Twenties. But they were only allowed to rent.

"It wasn't until the late Thirties that Mrs. Rindge allowed them to buy the land. Mrs. Rindge was having some money problems at that time. Many wealthy folks, especially celebrities began building then. That's when this house went up. Becky Wright and her architect husband built it. Oh, it's gone through numerous modifications and remodels over the years, but it's basically the same house."

"And how did Becky Wright die?" Even though it was broad daylight, Mrs. Goodman and her tales were scaring Kitty more than she'd have thought possible. Maybe it was just knowing that poor Mr. Evan had recently sat in the same chair that Mrs. Goodman sat in now. . .and died.

"Poisoned," said Mrs. Goodman without emotion. "Her

assistant found her dead in bed. They say she had a tortured look on her face. It must have been quite nasty."

"Did-did they ever find her killer?"

Mrs. Goodman shook her head. "No. Her husband was suspected, of course. Spouses always are."

"And what happened to him?"

"He disappeared. Then one day, his body washed up on the beach."

Kitty realized she was shivering.

"This beach right here. It was high tide and he washed up almost at the back doorstep. Eerie, isn't it?"

Kitty nodded.

Mrs. Goodman grinned. Kitty wondered if the woman enjoyed scaring her. "That was in 1940, I believe," said the doctor's wife. "The house sat empty for a spell, then went through several more owners. One of them was Desi Almodovar. They found him hanging from the rafters in what's now the study."

Kitty found her hands going to her neck and forced them back to the table. "Murdered?"

Mrs. Goodman shrugged. "Murdered, suicide, who knows? Again, I don't think the case was ever really solved. Though there was a lot of heat to do so. Almodovar was a very well known film director. He died in nineteen fifty-five. I remember because that's the year I was born."

"How do you know so much about the history of this place, Mrs. Goodman? Have you lived here very long?"

"Only five years or so. We lived in Pacific Palisades before that. Then Stephen decided he wanted to live at the beach and here we are. Personally, I hate all the sand. Gets into everything." She wiped her slacks.

"You ask how I know the history. One picks up gossip from the neighbors. People love to talk about the houses in the Colony as much as they do the occupants. And my husband is quite a history buff as well. The Wright house is quite famous, or should I say infamous?"

Mrs. Goodman rose and stared out the kitchen window. "There was a cult around Malibu back in the Twenties and Thirties—I don't know if they exist to this day—but they objected to the house being built on this spot."

"Why?" asked Kitty. "Were they trying to protect the beaches?"

"Nothing like that. You see," explained Mrs. Goodman, they believed this house was built on a lodestone—a lodestone that attracts evil energy from far and wide across the universe itself, drawing it in. . ."

Mrs. Goodman spun a hypnotic tale. "Day after day, hour after hour. Until the energy becomes too great, the stress too awesome." She turned and bore into Kitty with hard, flat eyes. "And when it becomes impossible, do you know what happens?"

Kitty shook her head, almost imperceptibly. She found herself incapable of taking her eyes away from Mrs. Goodman's face.

"The evil must escape." Mrs. Goodman's hand clenched tight. "And someone must die."

A wicked and taut silence filled the air.

Mrs. Goodman finally exhaled and grinned. "At least, that's what they say. But one would have to be crazy to believe the nonsense. Don't you think?"

Kitty forced herself to agree. "There were two more deaths. Wh-what about the others?"

Mrs. Goodman shrugged casually. "Tina Talbot. She was a soap star. She lived here in the seventies. Died around seventy-five, I believe. Poor thing was only twenty-six years old."

Though she wasn't certain she wanted to know, Kitty found herself asking, "How did Miss Talbot die?"

"Ah," said Mrs. Goodman, tapping her cheek. "Now that was an interesting one. Stephen often talks about it. It's the doctor/scientist in him, I suppose. You see, Tina Talbot was found in the middle of the living room. Burnt to death."

"There'd been a house fire?"

The woman was shaking her head. "Not even a living room fire. Only Tina Talbot burnt to a crisp. There wasn't a sign of a fire having come from or spread to anywhere else."

"Maybe she was smoking a cigarette or something and her clothing caught fire?"

"The coroner's report says she wasn't wearing clothes. She was naked." Mrs. Goodman laid her hand on Kitty's shoulder. Kitty could feel its icy coldness through the fabric of her shirt. "It was spontaneous combustion."

"But," said Kitty, "that's impossible."

"Tell that to Tina Talbot." Mrs. Goodman glanced at the gold watch on her wrist. "Oh, dear. I must be going. Stephen will be home soon. He won't like it that I'm at Rich's house."

"But Rich is dead, what does it matter?"

Mrs. Goodman shrugged. "I only know he won't like it."

Kitty rose and followed Mrs. Goodman as she bustled out the door. "But you never told me what happened to the fourth victim!"

Mrs. Goodman glanced at her house, seemed satisfied, and paused between Kitty and Consuelo's cars. "That was some entertainment attorney."

"A lawyer?"

"Yes. A Bruce Churchill, I believe. They say he blew his brains out all over the kitchen floor. His lover went mad. Totally mad." A long black Mercedes pulled into the Goodman drive and Mrs. Goodman ran to meet it.

# 15

Kitty glanced at her watch. At least she tried to, then realized she'd forgotten to wear it. She glanced at the microwave. It was time to go. She had an appointment with Angela Evan. When? Five minutes ago.

Why? She didn't know.

Since Angela Evan had a beach house in the Malibu Colony it was only a few minutes later when Kitty pulled into the drive of the ultra-modern, ultra-pink two story glass and concrete structure that Angela called home.

She rang the bell attached to a security camera setup and a moment later was rewarded with the buzz of an electronic lock being opened. Kitty pulled on the brass door handle and let herself in.

She half expected a robot to greet her but it was a young woman in a maid's uniform. Kitty gave her name and in exchange the maid led her to the deck out back where Her Highness was waiting in a chaise lounge.

Kitty stepped out into the sun and squinted. A cool breeze ruffled her hair. "You wanted to see me?"

"Yes, dear. I did. Thank you for coming by."

Kitty nodded. She'd been quite surprised when she'd checked her answering machine and found that message from Rich Evan's estranged wife asking her to come by today. "No problem."

Angela rose and went to the railing. A man and a woman jogged along the beach. The surf was low. Angela suddenly turned. "I'd like you to cook for me, dear."

"Cook for you?" That's what this is about? thought Kitty. This was the second time that someone had asked her to cook for them. "Sorry, I only cook for pets."

Angela was smiling patiently. "Yes, I know. And that's what I'd like you to do—cook for my pet. You do have an opening, don't you?"

Kitty nodded.

"I'll pay you your going rate."

Kitty looked around. "You have a pet?" She hadn't noticed anything four-legged running around when she'd come in. No barking, no meowing, no squawking. . .

"No," said Mrs. Evan, "not yet."

"But, then I don't understand—"

Angela patted Kitty's arm and Kitty felt her skin crawl. It was like rubbing up against a boa constrictor. Cool and slick. The image of Rich Evan in bed with Angela made her skin crawl all the more.

Angela explained. "I'd like you to handle that as well."

Kitty's brow furrowed. "What?"

"I'd like you to pick out a pet for me. Don't worry," said Angela, reaching for her purse on a small opaque glass table near the edge of the patio, "I'll pay you for your time." She withdrew some cash and held it out in her fine, tan fingers. "How does fifty dollars an hour sound?"

Kitty looked at the money then at Angela. "You want me to go to a pet store and pick you out a pet and then cook for it? Is that it?"

"Precisely," said Angela. She offered the money.

Kitty found herself taking the cash though the whole thing seemed goofy. "Is there any particular sort of pet that you'd like?"

Angela waved her hand. "Nothing too furry, dear. I abhor shedding. Gets into the furniture and the rugs. Very difficult to clean."

Kitty nodded her understanding though she had no doubt that Angela herself had never cleaned anything in her life with the exception of her own temple-like body.

And if Angela Evan had been an Egyptian queen in a previous lifetime, she wouldn't have even had to do that for herself. She'd have had servants to bathe her. For all Kitty knew, she had them doing it for her now.

Before Kitty could raise any further questions, Angela said, "Let me show you to the door."

As Angela was about to close said door in her face, Kitty asked, "Tell me, did Mr. Evan have any children?"

"Not with me he didn't."

"What about with any of his other wives?"

"No. Of course, Rich was always quite indiscriminate.

Like they say, 'Sex, drugs and rock and roll.' There may be a child or two born out of wedlock in the world. But I am not aware of any." Her eyes narrowed. "Why do you ask?"

"I was wondering who was going to inherit. You know, the house and all. Of course, if Mr. Evan didn't have any kids and the two of you were still married, well," said Kitty, batting her lashes, "I guess that means you'll inherit everything?"

Angela had her hand on the side of the door. "That's really none of your business, now is it?"

"No," replied Kitty, "of course not. I didn't mean to be nosy. It's just that I've heard a lot of stories about Mr. Evan's house being haunted or cursed or something and I wondered if you were intending to live in it?" Kitty raised an eyebrow. "I don't know about you, but you wouldn't catch me living in a place with a history like that."

"I have no intention of moving into Rich's house," Angela replied icily. "I'm quite happy here."

"I'll bet," Kitty said. "You've got a great house. Didn't it bother you living in a house where so many deaths had occurred?"

Angela merely shrugged. "I'd heard the stories. Not before I moved in, but after."

"And you weren't concerned?"

Angela smiled. "This town's full of stories. It's part of Hollywood's charm."

Kitty thought this an odd comment. "And you never noticed anything unusual while you lived there?"

"Only my husband's behavior," Angela deadpanned. "Now, if there is nothing further, I have a tennis lesson in half an hour."

"Of course." Kitty started away, then turned. "I wonder what made Mr. Evan get Benny?"

Angela sighed. "That's easy. Rich never had a pet, at least not while he was with me. But I know he was fond of dogs. Tracy knew it too and since she was obviously trying to get back in Rich's favor, she bought him a puppy as a present."

"Tracy? Do you mean his ex-wife Tracy?"

"That's right. Tracy Taylor Evan. She's an R&B singer. She came right before me in the marriage chain. If you ask me, she got tired of living in Rich's shadow. She wanted to be a star herself and couldn't compete with Rich's success and celebrity.

"I imagine she married him with the expectation that he would help her career, open doors for her, et cetera." Angela smiled. "But what she didn't know at the time was that Rich only worried about his own career. He wanted a little housewife to look pretty and cater to his every need. Tracy wanted the spotlight. From the stories I've heard, it turned into a real battle. By the time the divorce was settled, they loathed one another. For the longest time, it was forbidden to even mention Tracy's name."

Kitty nodded. "If everything was so horrible, why was Tracy trying to 'get back in his favor' as you say?"

"Easy," answered Angela. "Money. Rich had money and Tracy had none."

"Yet she must have had a good settlement."

"Rich had made her sign a prenup. She got two million. One for each year of their marriage."

That sounded pretty good to Kitty. More than enough to

last her a lifetime at any rate.

Angela read her mind. "Sounds like a lot to a person like you, doesn't it?"

Kitty ignored the slight. "Yes. It does."

"Well, Tracy went through it all pretty quickly. Spent it all in less than seven years."

Kitty whispered, "That doesn't seem possible."

"Lawyers, houses, cars, agents, promoters," said Angela. "It all adds up. Tracy was desperate to make herself a star. That takes money. And Tracy had run out of money and luck. She's been reduced to living in a one-room apartment in Van Nuys and waiting tables between singing jobs."

"That must be tough."

"That's when she started to worm herself back into Rich's life."

"How do you know all this, Mrs. Evan?"

"Rich and I separated nearly a year ago. But we were still on good terms and in touch with each other nearly daily."

"That's very civil. So many marriages end in such an ugly fashion."

"We were hoping for a reconciliation."

Somehow Kitty doubted Angela Evan wanted this. But what about Mr. Evan? Had he wanted her back?

"Rich told me that Tracy was pestering him constantly; phoning, writing him notes, sending emails."

"She wanted him back?"

"Tracy wanted his bank account back."

"Do you think she'll get anything now that he's dead?"

Angela glowered. "Not if I have anything to say about it."

Kitty thought hard. Tracy Evan could have murdered her

ex-husband even if there was no financial gain. Sheer spite would be enough to drive a person to murder. Revenge driven by the anger of seeing her ex-husband living better than she? Kitty's head throbbed. There were too many questions and not enough answers. "How about a bird?"

"I beg your pardon?"

"Would you like a bird?" repeated Kitty. "For a pet?"

"Hmmm," a finely manicured nail traced the bottom of her chin. "That would mean feathers, wouldn't it?"

Kitty swallowed her reply. Yeah, birds usually meant feathers—unless you planned on plucking, panning and plating them.

"I suppose," drawled Angela, "that would be all right. Would it talk?"

"You mean like a mynah bird or a parrot?"

"No, no. I mean like a person."

It took Kitty several moments to digest and decipher Angela's words. How could a woman who seemed so sharp and shrewd one moment appear so dumb and blonde the next?

Picking out a pet for Angela Evan wasn't going to be easy.

# 16

Kitty counted the bills before pushing them into her purse. Eleven hundred dollars. Maybe she'd buy Angela Evan a boa constrictor with all that cash. A boa constrictor with a gold choker chain.

She drove out to Ira and Iris Rabinowitz's home and delivered a late lunch to Goldie, their Pekingese. Today's luncheon was *The Doggie and the Hare.*

Kitty Karlyle Gourmet Pet Chef
—The Doggie and the Hare—

1/4 lb. boiled rabbit
1 tablespoon olive oil
1/8 cup finely chopped onion

*1 black olive*
*2 ounces white grape juice*
*1/4 teaspoon tomato puree*
*1 teaspoon lemon juice*
*1 artichoke*
*pinch kosher salt*
*hint of sage*
*1 sprig marjoram*

Kitty carefully set Goldie's plate on the floor with one of her recipe cards folded tent-like behind it. The Rabinowitz's were out, having left Kitty a note saying they'd gone to Temple.

Kitty knew where they kept the spare house key and they'd given her the alarm code, so this was no problem. In fact, it was a nice feeling to feel so trusted, especially in light of what had happened and all the troubles swirling around her.

Kitty waited until Goldie was finished and then removed the plate, washing it carefully in the sink and leaving it standing in the counter rack to dry.

She ran into a pet shop on Ventura Boulevard and picked up a get well card and a treat for Mr. Cookie. She didn't want to show up at the Randalls' empty-handed and that was where she was headed next.

At least she was until she realized how close Sherman Oaks was to Van Nuys. She pulled into a gas station, found a phone book and was, despite her low expectations, rewarded with an address for a Tracy T. Evan in Van Nuys.

Maybe she was in for a lucky streak. Not only had there been a Tracy Evan in the phone book, there had been a phone book. Usually the phone books were missing from the payphones or at best the pages were ripped out.

Kitty figured the old adage 'when you're hot, you're hot' was worth a shot. Without phoning ahead, she'd drop in on Rich Evan's ex-wife, Tracy, and hope to catch her at home. Besides, if she called first, the woman might not want to speak with her. It was better to approach in person.

Kitty found the address. It was a large old Moorish-styled apartment complex off Van Nuys Boulevard. The parking lot was filled up with derelict Seventies era large American automobiles mixed in with tiny later model foreign imports. She found an empty space between a humongous Buick and a small Honda Civic.

A quick scan of the register located beyond the busted security gate at the entrance revealed that Tracy T. Evan resided in apartment 312 East. After a few false turns, Kitty found the door leading to a third floor apartment facing west. The door was chipped and its paint faded. She knocked.

A small, black woman with an attractive face and large, liquid, cocoa-brown eyes, answered the door in her bathrobe. Wads of tissue were stuck between her freshly pink-painted toes and her left hand held a warm curling iron. "Can I help you?"

"Tracy Evan?"

"That's right."

"My name is Kitty Karlyle. I worked with Mr. Evan, Rich Evan." Kitty was forced to move as a six-foot, three hundred pounder, dressed like a Hell's Angel's attempted to squeeze past. He smelled of Old Spice and Old Milwaukee. "I was hoping I might have a word with you."

Tracy's eyes lit with hope. She smiled. "Sure, come on in. Don't mind the mess." She kicked newspaper out of her path and flopped down on a broken-down yellow and green striped sofa and motioned for Kitty to sit.

Kitty took the opposite edge of the sofa. The arm was covered in dog hair. It looked like Lhasa apso. She picked at a strand. "You have a dog?"

Tracy shrugged as she pulled the tissue out from between her toes. "Nah. Belongs to a friend. He spends a lot of time here." She balled up the used tissues in her fist and tossed them in the vicinity of a plastic trash can beside an electric keyboard on the wall opposite.

A dilapidated bookcase held a few tattered books and a CD collection. A poster from one of Tracy's gigs at a club in San Francisco had been tacked above it. "So, what is it you wanted to talk to me about?"

Kitty folded her hands in her lap. "Did you know that your ex-husband, Rich Evan, is dead?"

"Sure, I know. It's been all over the news." Her eyes scanned Kitty. "Are you a lawyer? Did Rich leave me anything?"

"Oh, no, nothing like that. I'm a cook."

"A cook?"

"That's right. I cooked meals for Mr. Evan's dog, Benny."

Tracy's eyes became hard. "Then what are you doing here? I don't need a cook. Couldn't afford one if I did." She waved around the tiny, old apartment for Kitty's benefit.

"This isn't exactly the Taj Mahal, as you can plainly see."

Kitty held her tongue. This place was worse than her own. It must be tough going from having it all to having next to nothing. "I was in the neighborhood and since—"

"Wait a sec. The cook, huh?" Tracy rose and pointed a finger at Kitty. "You're the one that's been in the news, too. They say Rich died because of something in the food that you prepared."

"It was an accident—I mean, I didn't put—"

Tracy stomped to the door and threw it open. "Get out."

Kitty stood. "But if you would just let me ask you a few questions."

"Get out now!"

All the way to Beverly Hills, Kitty couldn't help wondering if Tracy Evan was hiding something. Why else had she thrown her out without giving her a chance? Tracy Evan didn't really believe that Kitty had killed her ex-husband on purpose, did she? And Kitty had noticed a couple of *Milky Way* CDs in Tracy's collection. That was Fang Danson's band. Was there a connection between the two of them or was she merely reading more into it than there was? After all, Tracy had been married to Rich Evan and Fang was one of his best friends.

Then again, what if Tracy and Fang had conspired to kill Rich? What would they have had to gain? And how would they have known that Mr. Evan would eat the meal and not Benny?

# 17

"Gil is off for the evening," exclaimed Mrs. Randall, by way of explanation, as she pulled open the door leading into the kitchen.

Kitty immediately noticed Mr. Cookie lying in a large basket near the table. A small white and gold blanket covered his back. "How's Mr. Cookie?" she asked softly.

"He's fine. I trust you've followed Dr. Landau's orders to the letter?"

Kitty nodded. Before preparing any food for Mr. Cookie, she had been instructed to telephone the veterinarian for advice on diet and Mrs. Randall had insisted that he approve each meal until further notice. It was a pain in the backside but if this was what it took for Kitty to hold onto the job and keep Mr. Cookie and Mrs. Randall happy, then so be it.

"I've brought *Mr. Cookies and Cream.*" She pulled the

menu card from her slacks and handed it to Mrs. Randall.

"Hmmm," said Mrs. Randall, adjusting her glasses. "What is it precisely?"

"To tell the truth, it's chicken soup with milk." Mrs. Randall seemed dubious and Kitty added quickly, "Dr. Landau assured me it was ideal what with Mr. Cookie's tummy being sensitive yet."

Mrs. Randall hmm-hmmed some more. "I see." Her eyes scanned the ingredients. "None of this Barbados nut?"

Kitty shook her head vigorously.

"Fine," said Mrs. Randall with a wave of her upper class hand. "You may feed Mr. Cookie." She bent to pick up her precious cat. "I do hope this won't take long. My spiritualist is in the study."

"Spiritualist?" asked Kitty as she ritually placed the *Mr. Cookies and Cream* on Mr. Cookie's Wedgewood plate on Mr. Cookie's silver tray and ever so gently scooted the tray under Mr. Cookie's blue-blooded nose.

"That's correct. We're having a seance in less than an hour. We are attempting to contact several spirits from the past. Our home was over the years occupied by many celebrities and Madame Zouzou has quite the reputation for initiating contact with them. The spirits seem quite fond of her."

"I see." What Kitty really saw was that only the rich could afford such eccentricities.

"I'd like to have Mr. Cookie fed and in bed before the rest of my guests arrive."

Kitty said that would be no problem.

"That's interesting," said Kitty, laying out a linen napkin.

"I've been hearing quite a lot about spirits and ghosts and haunted houses myself lately. Have you ever heard of the Wright house out in Malibu?"

For a moment, Mrs. Randall seemed shaken. She recovered quickly and stood Mr. Cookie on the wooden table. "I am very familiar with the Wright home. Why do you ask?"

Kitty held her breath as the cat slowly steadied himself. True to form, Mr. Cookie looked at Mrs. Randall, who looked most concerned. He looked next at Kitty. True to her own form, Kitty wordlessly screamed for him to eat. Mr. Cookie sat back on his haunches, licked his whiskers, sniffed the air. . .

And slurped.

Kitty sighed. Success! Another day, another minor victory. "He likes it." She smiled at Mrs. Randall. True to her form, the old woman wasn't smiling back.

Kitty leaned against the counter and waited for Mr. Cookie to finish his dinner. "The Wright house belonged to Mr. Evan. That's where he—" she was going to say 'was killed' but stopped in the nick of time, "died."

Mrs. Randall's face blanched. "Rich Evan lived in the Wright house? How-how very odd." The old woman sat in the empty chair beside Mr. Cookie who was happily licking up his soup. She stroked his back. He gave her a glance then got back to work.

"Odd how, Mrs. Randall?"

Mrs. Randall looked at Kitty as if she'd forgotten the girl was there. "Mr. Randall and I used to know someone who lived in the Wright house." She was shaking her head. "But he died. . .many years ago. . ." Her voice trailed off.

Kitty felt a chill wind pass over her, as if an invisible and frigid spirit had passed through her body leaving her cold. Life was getting way too creepy these days. "Who was it, Mrs. Randall?"

"No one really. A friend of a friend. He was an attorney named Churchill."

Mr. Cookie meowed loudly, leapt from the table and flew out of the room.

A shiver surged up Kitty's spine. Her mouth was dry. "Bruce Churchill?" That was the entertainment attorney that Rich Evan's neighbor, Mrs. Goodman, had told her about. What had she said? He'd blown his brains out?

"Yes. He did some work for Mr. Randall."

"I heard Bruce Churchill was an entertainment attorney."

"Yes, I suppose he was. I mean, he could have been. I really didn't know much about him. I saw him once or twice. But as he was a friend of our other friend, he did give Mr. Randall some assistance on occasion." She pulled her fingers nervously.

"Who was this friend?"

Mrs. Randall shook her head. "That was many years ago. He wasn't even a friend really, more of an acquaintance. We lost touch. I can't even remember his name." She delicately pushed back her chair and rose. "I must join Madame Zouzou now."

Kitty gathered up her things and headed for the door. Mrs. Randall, quite out of character, laid her hand on Kitty's shoulder and leaned close. There was an odd sense of urgency in her voice as she spoke. "You must stay away from the Wright house, Miss Karlyle."

"Excuse me?"

Mrs. Randall's pupils sharpened to points. "It is an evil place. Evil things happen there."

Kitty tried to make light of it. "Don't worry. I could never afford to live there. The Malibu Colony is a bit out of my price range."

Kitty started to leave but Mrs. Randall still held the girl in her steely grip. "You must not enter the Wright house. Promise."

Kitty gulped. Mrs. Randall was close enough that she felt the old lady's breath on her face. She promised.

Mrs. Randall walked heavily through her large home looking for Mr. Cookie. She found him in the arms of Madame Zouzou. The spiritualist was sitting in a stiff-backed green velvet chair. Her long hair was balanced atop her head. She had a prominent, beak-like nose, of which she was rather proud. She said it helped her to sniff out the spirits.

Madame Zouzou was decked out in a flowing gold and purple frock. She'd removed her shoes as she always did. Madame Zouzou liked to be in contact with the earth, so she explained, as this provided a better chance of contacting the Dead.

Madame Zouzou looked up as Mrs. Randall came into the study. "The poor dear seems upset."

Mrs. Randall nodded. "Madame Zouzou, I must beg you to change tonight's goals somewhat."

Madame arched a brow. "How so, dear lady?"

"I need you to try to contact someone." She then uttered a name she had not uttered in years.

# 18

"I tell you, it was spooky, Velma." Kitty sat across from her bestfriend in one of the small booths along the side. Velma was on a break. The smells of Jack-In-The-Box, beef and fries largely, with overtones of high fructose corn syrup, filled the air and infiltrated Velma's hair and clothes.

"Sounds like it."

"I mean, I knew Mrs. Randall was odd, but you didn't tell me she was such a kook." Kitty had been so disturbed by recent events that she had driven all the way out to where Velma worked just to talk with her.

Velma smirked. She had a paperback novel in her hands. "The rich are all kooks. Didn't you know that, Kitty?"

Kitty nodded. "What's that you're reading?"

Velma held up the cover. "Freaky Flamingo Friday."

"Ooo-kay." Sounded goofy to her. "What's it about?"

Velma shrugged. "Some nut wearing an Al Gore mask is killing all the Florida mystery writers because he's angry that they write so many stories about what he calls freaks and geeks instead of normal people."

Kitty forced a laugh.

Velma fanned the book's pages. "He kills them by driving those pink flamingo yard ornaments through their chests."

"Huh?"

"You know, people stick them in the ground. They've got these stakes that you plant in the grass. He sharpens them up in his home shop and drives them through their hearts."

Kitty felt like she was going to be sick and said so. "Is the book any good at all?"

"Nah, it sucks." Velma slammed the novel down on the table.

"So why do you keep reading it?"

"So I can tell everybody how bad it is. I'm going to post the info on my Amazon link."

Kitty remembered Velma explaining how she used to review mystery novels back in Michigan and post them on the Internet. "I thought you gave up reading mysteries?"

Velma heaved her shoulders. "Yeah, but I started again. Gives me something to do on my breaks."

Kitty nodded. "Makes sense." Reading books you can't stand. "I guess."

Velma sucked up her diet Coke. "You want anything?"

Kitty shook her head.

"It's free."

"No thanks. Say, I have to go pick out a pet for a client. Want to come with me?"

A man in a paper hat, the manager, suspected Kitty, yelled at Velma to get back to work. Velma waved him off.

"Sure," said Velma. "My shift's only half over but it's no big deal. It's dead tonight, anyway." She scooped up her purse and book, leaving her trash on the table. "Hey, Glen, I'm leaving."

The manager had his hand in the register. "What do you mean you're leaving?" he hollered.

Velma patted her not inconsequential stomach. "I'm not feeling so good. I must be sick."

He glowered. "You were fine a little while ago."

Velma stared him down. "It must be the food then."

"Vel!" whispered Kitty, "be careful before you get yourself fired."

"Don't worry about it," Velma said. "Did I tell you I've got an interview at Orleans on Doheny? Wait here while I go punch out."

Kitty was impressed. Orleans was a fairly new four-star restaurant owned by one of the city's oldest restaurant families. Getting a chef's position there would be just the thing that Velma needed.

"So, a pet, eh?" Velma padded along beside Kitty. They'd taken Kitty's car to a pet shop in West L.A. that Kitty knew kept late hours. "Who's it for?"

Kitty explained.

Velma reached into a wired cage near the doors that contained some rabbits. She grabbed a small white bunny and lifted it up. She rubbed her nose against the bunny's. "So, Rich Evan's ex-wife has no pet and she gives you over a thousand dollars to buy her one and then she's going to pay you to cook for it."

"Yep."

Velma set the bunny gently back into the cage. "Seems pretty strange, if you ask me."

"I am asking you. I mean. It's so weird. You know, I thought I'd start losing clients after what happened to poor Mr. Evan, instead Fang Danson has asked me to cook for Benny and now Angela Evan has asked me to cook for her pet." Kitty scanned the aisles of fish. "After I find her one, that is."

"Listen, Kitty, being an accused murderess, even if it isn't true and only lasts one day, that kind of makes you a celebrity in this town. And that's the only coin that matters."

"Oh, Velma. You're too cynical. But underneath that crusty exterior, I know you don't mean half what you say."

"Huh!" grunted Velma, as if affronted. "I prefer to keep my crust intact, thank you very much. As for your troubles, Kitty, I expect they are fading fast."

"I don't know about that. I talked to that detective. The police don't seem any closer to solving the murder than they were in the beginning. And somebody tried to poison Mr. Cookie and it might have been with the same Barbados nut that killed Mr. Evan."

"Rich Evan's murder," Velma said sharply, "is old news. The Middle East is boiling over, the Chechens are on the warpath and the market is down. Nobody cares about the murder of an aging rock star anymore. It's all going to fade away. Just you wait and see. Your biggest problem is going to be what to feed all the rich little dogs and cats this season.

Some days, I wish I was a pet so you could cook for me."

"Please, you're a terrific chef yourself."

"Yeah, I'm sure Jack-In-The-Box appreciates my talents."

"Hey, come on, cheer up. You've got that interview with Orleans set up, haven't you?"

"Tomorrow. Wish me luck."

Kitty did. She pulled Velma's sleeve as they maneuvered around a pallet loaded sky high with fifty-pound sacks of dog food. "Oh, and did I mention that Fang Danson also asked me if I'd be interested in cooking for him personally?"

"Yeah, right." Velma veered right. "It's a ploy."

"What do you mean a ploy?"

"I mean he's probably only trying to get in your pants."

Kitty nodded. Memories of her previous encounters with Fang Danson played through her mind. "You could be right."

Velma suddenly grinned and rapped her knuckles on a wooden kennel near the cash register. "How about a pig?"

Kitty giggled. A lonely looking gray and black speckled Vietnamese pot-bellied pig stood all alone in a large pen. "Oh, no, I couldn't. Could I?"

Velma clapped and the pig rubbed his snout in her hands. "If you ask me, it's perfect. This Angela Evan sounds like a real pig herself."

Kitty studied the pig. There had been a time when they were all the rage in L.A. And pigs were said to be quite intelligent.

The pig was licking Velma's fingers. "You think they allow pigs in the Colony?" Velma asked over her shoulder. "Of course," she said, answering her own question, "they allow two-legged pigs, so why shouldn't they allow the four-legged kind?"

"I think I'd better keep looking."

"Suit yourself." Velma wiped her hands on her slacks and followed Kitty past the dog cages.

"These puppies are so adorable, but I don't think Ms. Evan would like a pet that she considered to be too much trouble."

"Like she's going to do any of the work herself," quipped Velma. "She's got you to feed it and she'll get someone else to walk it and someone else yet again to clean up after it."

Kitty said nothing. Velma was probably right, after all. Definitely right. "A cat, you think?"

"Fur, hairballs," Velma said flatly. "Litter boxes."

Kitty nodded and moved on. "How about some fish?"

"Sure, I could use a bite to eat."

"I meant for Ms. Evan."

"I know, I was joking. Fish sound like they'd be right up her alley."

Kitty tapped her lip. "Boring though. I had told her I might get a bird."

"Great," said Velma, leading Kitty on. "I saw some this way."

"Did I tell you that I saw that detective again?"

"What detective?"

"Det. Young, the one who interviewed me when Mr. Evan died. You'll never believe what he told me."

Velma turned her head and planted her hands on her broad hips. "Well?"

"He told me he was going to marry me." Kitty felt herself flushing and wasn't sure why.

Velma's face expressed incredulity. "He what? Are you serious? No, you're joking—"

Kitty emphatically shook her head no. "I kid you not."

Velma resumed walking. "It just goes to prove what they say. This town is Granolaville. Plenty of fruits, nuts and flakes. Not surprising that even a policeman can be nutty. They can't keep them all off the force."

Velma stopped in front of a cage filled with squawking parrots. "Take your pick."

Kitty stepped past Velma. "That one." The one she was pointing to was in a brass cage all alone. And it wasn't a parrot, it was an Australian cockatiel.

Velma nodded. "Hey, this is the same kind of bird that those two fellows, Richard and Timothy, had. I saw it that day I went with you on your rounds."

Kitty smiled. "Exactly. And since I've got to cook for one cockatiel, it'll be just as easy to prepare meals for two."

Velma smiled back. "Saves you having to come up with separate dishes for parrots and cockatiels."

"You got it."

"Girl, you're finally beginning to use your brains. Now let's go get this critter rung up and get some fish—broiled this time and lightly seasoned."

They left the store with the bird and all the basic trimmings, cage, conditioner, a book on bird care and even some bird food. Kitty figured it wouldn't hurt for Angela to read up on birds nor to have a little food in stock for snacks and emergencies.

Velma had wanted Kitty to pick *Cockatiels For Dummies*, but Kitty wouldn't dare have given it to Ms. Evan and selected *Schmidt's Complete Cockatiel Care* in its stead. She also had a handful of cash left over which Velma thought they should spend on dinner but Kitty insisted on returning to Ms. Evan.

"Sometimes," said Kitty, "I think I should just give up." They sat out-of-doors at a small seafood restaurant along Santa Monica's boardwalk. It was quite cool and the fog had settled in. Nonetheless, she yawned.

Velma drained her second glass of Cabernet. "What we ought to do," she said, "is open our own restaurant. I mean, we'd make a great team."

Kitty nodded.

"And look how well your folks do."

Kitty caught a yawn in the palm of her hand. "Sorry. Hey, speaking of my folks, I'm going down to see them tomorrow, want to come?"

"Can't," said Velma, shaking her head, "I'm going to have to make up some hours at work. What are you going down there for?"

"Ever since this murder they've been bugging me to come down. They're so busy with the restaurant, it's hard for them to get away. Besides, I want to go see Aunt Gloria."

"The librarian?" Velma wiped up the last of the tartar sauce with a cold french fry.

"Yeah. I haven't seen her in ages. I miss her." Aunt Gloria was such a great spirit. Just what Kitty needed. "And she's terrific at looking stuff up. She'll be able to help me come up with some recipes for the birds." The caged cockatiel in question occupied the chair beside Kitty. She'd draped her sweater over the bird to keep him warm and so far he wasn't complaining.

Kitty lowered her voice. "Speaking of spirits," she began, "did you know that Mrs. Randall was into spirits?"

Velma shrugged halfheartedly. "No. How would I know that?"

"Well, she is. I was there earlier this evening. She told me she was going to have a seance."

"Granolaville, redux. Too much money and too much free time. Maybe the old lady should get a job. Jack-In-The-Box always has openings, especially on the late shift."

"The strange thing is, I've been hearing a lot about ghosts and haunted houses lately—ever since poor Mr. Evan was murdered."

Kitty expounded on all she had been told by Fang Danson, Mrs. Goodman, Consuelo and others. "There's something weird about all those people dying in strange ways in that house.

"And when I mentioned the Wright house to Mrs. Randall, she practically turned white as a sheet. It turns out she knew someone who'd lived in the Wright house before, an attorney named Bruce Churchill. Isn't that a funny coincidence, Vel?"

"I'll say." Velma had stopped chewing. "What else did she have to say?"

"Not much. She didn't seem to want to talk about it." Kitty tapped the table with her knife. "But I think she knows something. . .something that she isn't telling."

There was a pregnant silence. A lone, thin male on in-line skates streaked by like a ghost along the near desolate boardwalk.

Velma forced a laugh. "Hey, come on. Let's get out of here," she said. "All this crazy talk. Guys blowing their brains out. You're beginning to spook me, Kitty. I mean, next you'll be telling me that you believe in evil spirits and ghosts and stuff and that some malevolent force killed Rich Evan."

Kitty bit her cheek. "Do you think it's possible?" she whispered. "Could the Wright house have been built on this lodestone of evil Mrs. Goodman mentioned? Is the house possessed?"

# 19

"It's you." Fang stood in the doorway in a pair of purple boxer shorts, his blue robe half-opened, revealing a lightly haired chest. A lit cigarette danced between his lips.

Tracy Taylor Evan tossed him the thick Sunday L.A. Times that she'd picked up from his drive. "Brought you your paper."

Fang grunted a thanks and Tracy didn't wait for him to invite her inside. She gave him a brief hug and, still holding him close, said, "I had someone nosing around my apartment complex yesterday, asking questions."

"A cop?"

Tracy shook her head. She looked stunning in a pair of cotton/spandex low-cut jeans and matching top, and knew it. "No, some girl. About my age. Said she was a chef—that she cooked for that dog I gave Rich, if you can believe it."

Maybe because he had heard his name, Benny came running up. He sniffed Tracy's sandals then eased out the front door in search of new adventure.

"Benny? You've got the dog?" Tracy said in disbelief.

"That's right. I'm looking after him now."

"And that girl is Kitty Karlyle and she does the meals for Benny here at Fang's house, doesn't she, darling?" Angela Evan, a study in cool sophistication in a pure white satin robe strolled royally into the foyer.

Tracy quickly let go of Fang and retreated a step. "Hi, Angie. You know that girl?"

Angela nodded. "I just said I did, didn't I?" Angela planted a slow kiss on Fang's stubbled cheek. "You came all the way out to Santa Monica just to tell Fang about your visit with a dog cook? It would have been so much simpler to telephone."

Angela was nearly sneering. "You can still afford a telephone, can't you, dear?"

Tracy looked ready to dismember the woman. "Fang asked me to come over, *Angie, dear.*"

"Oh?" Angela was looking at Fang now.

"I asked her to come over and double up her vocal track on *When The Summer Comes*," explained Fang.

"Fine." Angela was casting a suspicious look at Tracy. "I'll have Derrick bring us up some coffee." If Tracy thought she was going to sink her claws into Fang, she had another thing coming.

As Fang warmed up the recording gear, Tracy wrapped her hands around a cup of coffee made nearly white with cream. "What should I do if this Karlyle girl comes around again? I mean, she was asking me questions about Rich's death. What am I supposed to tell her if she asks again?"

"What did you tell her this time?" Angela's voice was cool as ice.

"Nothing. I threw her out."

"And that's exactly what you'll do if she bothers you again." Angela set her own empty cup on the floor. "But I don't believe she will."

"What have you got in mind?" said Fang, turning his head, while his hands played over the recording console.

Angela shrugged and tugged at her lounging robe. "I think that Ms. Karlyle merely needs to be kept busy."

"Like you telling her to get you a pet?" Fang laughed. "Hard to imagine you with a pet."

Angela raised a telling eyebrow. "I've taken good care of you, haven't I, darling?"

"Very funny," replied Fang.

Angela went on. "We keep Kitty Karlyle occupied. And if she is occupied, she will be too busy to ask questions. It's that simple. Ask your friends to hire her to cook for their pets, Fang. I've already begun doing the same. We'll make Kitty Karlyle the most successful pet chef in the business. She'll be too busy making money to make trouble." Angela smiled at her own wit.

"And if that doesn't stop her?" pressed Tracy, running her finger nervously along the edge of her cup.

Angela smiled cooly in Tracy's direction. "Maybe you'll be a dear and kill her for us."

"Kill—" Tracy dropped her cup. It fell to the floor, spilling coffee all over the carpet.

Fang shouted angrily and buzzed Derrick on the intercom to come and sop it up.

"You can't be serious?" Tracy was gaping.

Angela shrugged. "Why not? People O.D. in this town everyday, don't they? Surely you must have some connections. I've heard a speedball can do the trick."

Tracy bit her lower lip and glowered at Angela. "I've been clean for over a year," she hissed.

"Of course you have, dear." Angela's sarcasm and scorn sounded two feet thick.

Tracy stormed out.

Fang sighed. "You shouldn't have done that, Angela. We need her."

Angela crossed her arms. "She needs us more."

# 20

"Kitty, you look wonderful."

"Thank you, Aunt Gloria." Kitty squeezed Aunt Gloria hard. "So do you." Kitty's aunt, her mother's sister, was head librarian in the City of San Diego Public Library system and Kitty adored her. Kitty believed librarians like teachers, culinary or otherwise were about the greatest and she held them all in high esteem.

Aunt Gloria swept a lock of blonde hair from her round face. "So, you went to see your parents?"

"Yes. They said to say hello and send their love."

"I haven't seen Mark and Paula in over a month, not since Jay's birthday." Jay was Aunt Gloria's son.

"They must be quite worried about you. This Rich Evan murder even made the papers here. The library was buzzing over it for a few days. Don't tell anyone I said this, but even librarians can be quite gossipy at times."

Kitty nodded. "Mom and Dad keep telling me to come home for a while."

"Maybe you should." She held her niece at arm's length. "You look tired."

"But I've just gotten my pet chef business off the ground. If I stop now, it'll spell the end of it. Not that I don't sometimes think that's just what I should do. If it doesn't fail anyway. If the police don't find Rich Evan's real killer soon, I'll be facing the reputation of the chef who kills pets and their owners."

Aunt Gloria pushed her reading glasses up her nose and told her niece not to worry. "We'll get to the bottom of this." Kitty wished this was true but she'd read enough news over the years to know that not every crime could be solved. And if this one wasn't. . .

Aunt Gloria told Kitty to follow her and the two ladies retired to her office in the corner of the children's department. Aunt Gloria made a note of the poison that Kitty mentioned. "You know me," she explained, "I like to research and I'm curious about this poison and how it might have interacted with the other drugs that the police say were in Mr. Evan's system. Is this Barbados nut considered poisonous to pets?"

Kitty told her how Mrs. Randall's cat, Mr. Cookie, had also been poisoned and nearly faced death himself.

"How curious."

Kitty, anxious to change the subject from the dead to the living, explained how she'd recently taken on some new clients, including two with birds and needed some interesting cockatiel recipes.

"That shouldn't be too much trouble. I believe we even have several books on bird care and feeding here in the system. I'll take a look for you and send you up anything appropriate that I find."

"Thank you, Aunt Gloria." Angela Evan's cockatiel was spending Sunday at her apartment. She would take it to the woman tomorrow, first chance she got. Having the bird in the house was driving her cat, Barney, nuts. "I don't know what I'd do without your help. Without everyone's help."

Her aunt smiled. "You'd do just fine, dear. You're quite capable and don't let anyone tell you otherwise."

She leaned over her desk and took Kitty's hand. "Now, young lady, capable as you are, I can see right through you. You did not drive all the way down to San Diego from Los Angeles on your only day off just to ask me about bird food recipes. We could have handled this on the telephone. What is it? What's on your mind?"

"It's this Rich Evan murder," sighed Kitty. "Nothing about it makes sense. I mean, it seems as though someone was actually trying to kill Benny and poor Mr. Evan got killed instead." Kitty hesitated, glancing at her aunt, then the floor. Finally, she said, "It's almost as if the stories are true."

"Stories?" Aunt Gloria asked. "What stories?"

"About Mr. Evan's house being haunted."

"Haunted?" Kitty's aunt looked skeptical.

"Or evil." Kitty shook her head. "I don't know. I realize it must sound silly—"

Aunt Gloria built a tall steepled church out of her fingers. "Oh, I don't know about that. There's been a lot of literature about," she searched for the words she wanted, "spiritual emanations, vortexes of weird energy and other unusual and unexplained phenomena. We've an entire section devoted to such things here in the library. The paranormal."

"Exactly!" cried Kitty. "You wouldn't believe half the weird things that have happened in that house."

Aunt Gloria grabbed a pencil. "Tell me more about these stories, Kitty."

Kitty left the library lighter of heart and with renewed determination. Aunt Gloria was not only going to help her with the bird food recipes, she'd promised to research the old Wright house and its occupants. Kitty had given her aunt all the names she could remember. Aunt Gloria was confident she could uncover the names of the rest.

After seeing her niece off, Gloria Casselberry headed to the reference section to check on some things that Kitty had mentioned. On the way, she passed the news racks where the day's papers were kept. The headline of the *San Diego Times* caught her eye. *DEPT. STORE CHAIN WIFE FOUND DEAD.*

The librarian pulled the paper off the rack and read. Mrs. Lucille Randall, wife of Henry Randall, founder of the Randall Department Store chain, had been found dead in her home, strangled. Was this the same Mrs. Randall with the cat who'd been poisoned that Kitty had mentioned earlier? How odd for her niece not to have mentioned this. Perhaps she didn't know? She'd better give Kitty a call.

Just then a patron tugged on the librarian's arm searching

for a copy of *Books In Print* and Gloria Casselberry's attention turned to more immediate concerns.

"Well," grumbled Fang, "now that you've chased Tracy out of here and I'm not likely to get any work done, I'd might as well read the paper." He carried the newspaper out to the backyard and settled down to read. He ordered Derrick to bring him some breakfast.

A few minutes later, Angela appeared, dressed in an anil blue leotard with a bare midriff. She leapt down to the lawn and began doing stretches. She warmed up with a Trikonasana—the triangle, one of the easier poses her yoga instructor, Jean-George, had taught her.

Fang unfolded the paper. A line appeared in his forehead. "What the—"

Angela stopped mid-pose. "What is it?"

Fang lowered the paper. "It says here that Lucille Randall has been murdered."

"Really?" giggled Angela, dropping into a lotus position. The grass was damp. She should have brought an exercise mat. "I hope it wasn't something she ate."

"What's that supposed to mean?"

"The Randalls were clients of Kitty Karlyle's Pet Gourmet service."

"How do you know that?"

"Don't you remember?" sighed Angela, wondering why she stuck with such a dolt—Rich was a certified genius compared to Fang—"Rich let them use a song of his for a radio and TV ad campaign."

She went from a Bhujangasana—the cobra— to an Adho

Mukha Svanasana, carefully synchronizing her breathing with her movements. Her rear lifted upward, like a gift, and Fang was of a mind to take it.

"Henry Randall recommended Miss Karlyle to Rich when Tracy gave him that damn puppy." Angela turned her head. She was beaming. "And now Randall's wife is dead. Isn't it wonderful?"

"What's so wonderful about it? What's her death got to do with us?"

Angela rose and sauntered over to the table where Derrick had just delivered Fang his breakfast, eggs, sausage and toast. "It means that the police will be locking up Kitty Karlyle sooner rather than later. The Rich Evan case will be solved. The lawyers will get the courts moving and I'll get my settlement."

Fang grumbled.

"It seems our pet chef is a serial poisoner." Angela rubbed Fang's shoulders. "Speaking of which, you haven't touched your breakfast."

Fang pushed his plate away. Angela was making him uneasy. "Killer or not, Kitty Karlyle didn't poison Lucille Randall."

"She didn't?"

Fang reveled in Angela's confused look. "That's right," he said, smacking the paper. "It says here the old woman was strangled."

"Strangled?" muttered Angela, clenching her fist.

# 21

"Where are you?"

Where Kitty was right at that most difficult moment was entering Interstate 5 in San Diego. Where she was heading was back home. What she needed were two hands free to grip the steering wheel. What she didn't need was a call on her cell phone. Now of all times. This of all people.

"How did you get this number?" she shouted into the phone, ignoring his question. A trucker shot past her and the Volvo shook. There was a giggle at the other end of the line.

"A little bird told me," Det. Young said. "And you haven't answered my first question."

"A little bird? How did you know about the bird?"

"What bird? Where are you?"

"San Diego. Now is there a reason for this call or are you simply trying to get me killed trying to merge with seventy-mile-an-hour traffic while shooting the breeze with you?"

"Boy, you're pretty snappy today. And on your day off," Young said. "Not getting enough sleep?"

"How do you know this is my day off?"

"So what are you doing in San Diego?"

Kitty stared at the phone then practically stuck it in her mouth as she settled into the slow lane. "What? Are you afraid I may be making a break for the Mexican border, detective? Pet chef escapes justice in Tijuana?"

"Are you done?" He waited and since she said nothing he pushed ahead. "Actually, the reason I was calling was to invite you on our second date. But it might not work out now. I mean, if you're all the way down in—"

Her scream pierced his ear. "Excuse me?! Second date? When exactly was our first date?"

"Hey, what do you mean? I mean, that really hurts. I went with you to visit your sick client. If that doesn't qualify as a first date, I don't know what does. I mean, I did that totally for you—how thoughtful and modern can a guy get?"

"My sick . . ?" Kitty's head was throbbing. If only she had an aspirin. She ground her fist into her temple, it was the next best thing. "You mean Mr. Cookie?"

"Yeah, that's the guy."

There was silence at her end.

"So? What do you think? What time will you get back? We can meet at your apartment, or better still, I know a great little place at the edge of Beverly Hills." He named a place on Little Santa Monica Boulevard that was popular with the locals. It was also one of the cheapest. "You could meet me there." Young looked at his watch. "In two hours?"

Kitty had to unclench her jawbones to manage an answer. If she had been any angrier, it would have taken the Jaws of Life to unlock them.

Oh, she'd meet him there all right. And she'd give Jack Young a piece of her mind that he would never forget.

She had to park a block away and even then had to squeeze into a parking space foreshortened by the cars sticking out in front and in back. Not to mention that parallel parking was not one of her best talents. She ignored the parking meter and headed to Augy's Restaurant.

Kitty blundered past a server balancing a loaded tray. "Excuse me," she uttered. She spotted her quarry seated at a small table near the window. The detective was wearing his brown suit again and apparently no one had told the man to stop wearing black loafers with brown clothes. To make matters worse, he'd chosen white socks. He was reading the newspaper and didn't see her coming.

"You have a lot of nerve!" she began loudly. "First that nonsense the other day telling me how you are going to *marry* me and calling me up and talking like we're going to have a second date." Her face was purplish and her cheeks bulged. "When you *know* very well we've never had a *first* date." She was shaking her head and her body followed along as she bounded on the soles of her feet. "Like I would *ever* go out with you—"

"Hi, Kitty. Great to see you again, too." He looked up and he was smiling.

"There is absolutely nothing funny about this. And I want you to know that I find your behavior despicable." She ignored the stares of the other patrons and the ugly glare of the staff.

Det. Young slowly laid down the sports section, rummaged around in the thick pile of paper on the table, dug up the front page and held it up. "Seen the paper today?"

"Are you out of your mind?" She was clearly flabbergasted. Her eyes glanced at the paper. "Haven't you even heard anything that—" What the? "—I—" Mrs. Randall? Dead? It couldn't be! "—said?"

Kitty's shoulders slumped. She looked at the detective for answers.

He rose and pulled out the chair opposite his. "Have a seat." He pushed her up to the table. "I'll order us some drinks. How about a Mimosa? I hear it's the specialty here."

Kitty merely nodded. The drinks arrived. She raised her glass and sipped slowly. It seemed to carry a subtle hint of cranberry in addition to the orange juice. She'd scanned the front page that Det. Young had laid before her. He watched her in silence.

Finally, she looked up at him. "Is this what this was all about? The phone call? The second date?"

He looked back at her as if she was speaking Martian.

"It was all a trick, wasn't it? You only wanted to question me about Mrs. Randall's death." She pushed back her chair. "Do you think I killed her, too?"

The manager rushed over. "Is everything all right?" He looked about nervously.

"Yes, fine." Det. Young assured the manager it was nothing and he left.

Kitty fumed. "You're sick, you know that?"

"Are you done?"

She glared.

"Fine. Then you can listen for a change. I asked you here because I really did want to see you again."

"Sure, so you can lock me up. Tell me, will they give you a shiny medal for your shirt?"

"I thought you were going to let me talk?"

Kitty drummed the table with her fingers.

"I wanted to see you—" He appeared to fumble for the word. "Socially. The rest is mere coincidence. I read about Lucille Randall's death in the paper just like you did."

Kitty felt herself softening. "You mean, you only found about it now yourself?"

"Well, no. I read about it this morning. I put in a call to the Beverly Hills Police Department and inspected the scene."

"So this *is* an interrogation."

He swirled his drink. "I guess it was stupid. I thought I could kill two birds with one stone as they say. See you again, socially, and ask you about Lucille Randall's murder."

Kitty laughed out loud. "I don't believe you." She was shaking her head. "So this is like a combination date and third degree interrogation? Clever. And charming. You must be quite popular with the ladies, detective."

"It's Jack, remember?" He tugged at his skinny brown tie. "And I've done just fine, thank you."

"I'll bet." Kitty folded her arms. "Are we done here?"

"Look," he leaned across the table, "I'm sorry. It was a dumb idea." He cleared his throat. "I really am sorry. How about if we order some lunch and start over?"

Kitty winced. This did not sound like such a good idea.

"Please?" He picked up the newspaper and tossed it on the floor. "We don't even have to talk about the investigation or police business or anything."

"So what do we do? Sit and stare at one another? This isn't going to work. We have nothing in common and absolutely nothing to talk about."

"Oh, I don't know." Young smiled. "I know. We can talk about pets. Let's take dog food, for instance. I've been buying Libby the Alpo. But Walmart's got an unbeatable price on Ole Roy."

"Would you like it if you belonged to someone and they fed you solely out of cans?"

The detective shrugged. "I don't think I'd mind. Sure, why not? Plenty of good food comes in cans."

"Name two."

Young scratched an ear. "Spaghetti, soup."

"Oh, brother."

His eyes lit up. "Beef stew. I love beef stew. Ever have Dinty Moore's?" He picked up the menu. "I wonder if they've got that here."

Kitty watched the detective as he read the menu. Though she'd only had a slice of toast and a glass of milk for breakfast, she had little appetite. "Tell me what happened to Mrs. Randall, Jack," she said softly.

He lowered his menu and looked into her eyes. "There isn't a whole lot to tell yet. Her husband came home early this morning and found her dead on the floor of the study."

"He was gone all night? Isn't that odd? Could he have killed her himself?" Henry Randall was such a serene and soft-spoken man generally. She really couldn't imagine him strangling his wife. But one never knew. The mere thought sent shivers up her spine.

"No, he's in the clear. He was out of town on business and caught the redeye back. Tons of witnesses can place him in Spokane. He's opening up a new store there."

This was good news. "And there are no clues?"

He shook his head. "And no witnesses."

"What about Gil?"

"Who?"

"The houseman."

"Oh, him. He was off for the evening."

"That's right," replied Kitty. "I remember Mrs. Randall telling me that."

"When did you see her last?"

"Yesterday evening when I took Mr. Cookie his dinner."

"How's the cat doing?"

"Much better." And now Mrs. Randall was dead. "I don't know if this will be of any help, but Mrs. Randall was holding a seance last night at her home."

Young chuckled. "A seance? Like with crystal balls and incense?"

"I guess."

"So she had guests. Do you have any names?"

"No." Kitty shook her head. "Wait. The clairvoyant or spiritualist or whatever—Mrs. Randall told me her name." Kitty closed her eyes and thought. "Madame Zouzou." She opened her eyes. "Yes, that was it."

Young twisted his lower lip. "Hmmm, the police will want to have a word with her. Not that it's likely that Lucille

Randall got strangled by a ghost. . ."

This was the opening Kitty had hoped for. "Actually. . ."

"Don't tell me you believe in ghosts?" He was smirking.

"Of course not." Kitty snatched up her menu and studied her choices. "Do you?"

"Do I what?"

"Do you believe in ghosts?"

His answer came quickly and firmly. "No. I did have a great-aunt once who used to tell ghost stories. Some of them were real wild. This was back in the Ozarks where I grew up. But she's gone now."

"What happened to her?"

"She burned down her farm house one day because she was sure it was haunted. They locked her up after that in an assisted care facility and one day she died."

"I've heard that the Wright house is haunted." Kitty ordered the artichoke pizza. Young ordered the same.

"What's the Wright house?"

"That's the house Mr. Evan owned. It's known as the Wright house."

"Why's that?"

Kitty explained as best she could.

"And you think that all of this—" He waved his fork around in the air. "—Everything weird that's been going on is related to this vortex of evil or something?"

"You said it yourself, Jack. Weird things have been happening. What if it is somehow related to some sort of odd and malevolent supernatural manifestation?"

The detective laughed. To Kitty it sounded like false bravado. Maybe he was only trying to frighten off any ghosts that might be listening in.

"Come on," he chided. "This is nutty. Rich Evan was poisoned. Lucille Randall was strangled. They were murdered by flesh and blood people, *human beings*," he said with emphasis. "Not by spooks."

"But—"

"Besides," he went on, "Mrs. Randall was not murdered in the Wright house. She was killed in her own home. Are you forgetting that?"

Kitty shook her head no.

"And all we have to do is find the motives behind their murders. Find the motives, find the killers. It's that simple, Kitty. Trust me."

"If it's so simple, why haven't the police found the motive behind even Mr. Evan's murder yet?"

Young snapped off the end of a pizza slice and chewed hard. "Money, sex, jealousy, insanity maybe," he rattled off. "Those are your typical motives. All we've got to do is figure out which applies."

"Okay, let's take money, for instance. I heard Mr. Evan had no children."

"That appears to be the case."

"So how about family?"

Young shook his head and polished off his lunch, washing it down with ice water. He dabbed his lips with a paper napkin. "You gonna finish that?" he asked, eying a roll on the edge of her plate.

She pushed it his way. She watched him shovel it into his mouth.

He gobbled it up and wiped his mouth once again.

"Sorry," he apologized, "I haven't eaten since yesterday."

Kitty rolled her eyes. This guy was too much trouble. "I was asking if Rich Evan had any family."

"Right. Nope."

"None?"

"Not a soul. Rich Evan was an orphan. Born in England, raised by a couple who'd adopted him at birth."

"So there's them—the couple who'd adopted him. Even though Mr. Evan was still legally married to Angela Evan, wouldn't they also be entitled to a share of his estate?" And Rich Evan had to be worth millions.

Young was shaking his head again. "Both dead. Rich Evan had no other next-of-kin."

"So everything goes to Angela Evan. . ."

"Maybe. But it's all pretty messy legal-wise. Rich and Angela had been separated for a year and were in the process of getting a divorce."

"She says they were hoping to reconcile."

"That's not what Rich Evan's divorce attorney says. He also says Rich and Angela had a prenup."

Kitty nodded. "That makes sense. I heard he'd made the same arrangement with his prior wife, Tracy. She got something like a million dollars for each year they stayed married."

Young whistled. "Not a bad deal. I think I could put up with just about anyone for a year and a million dollar payoff."

"There must be some other suspects. . ."

"Besides you, you mean?" He grinned. "Sorry, only joking. There are all sorts of suspects. Ex-wives, business associates, like Fang Danson. Drug dealers. The world is full of suspects. Then again, maybe he only accidently ate the dog's food."

"Still, someone had to put the poison in Benny's breakfast. Maybe it was the housekeeper. She certainly had the most access."

"What's her motive? He wouldn't give her a raise? And was Consuelo out to kill him or warn him by killing his dog?"

"It could have been either. She didn't seem overly fond of her employer. Mr. Evan had promised to help Consuelo's brother and father come into the country, so she claims. And it seems he reneged on this. So she goes nuts and kills him or intended to kill Benny to hurt him like she believes he has hurt her—"

Young shrugged. "We'll check it out. It seems to me you know too much."

"What's that supposed to mean?"

"It means stop snooping around and leave the police work to the police."

"If I do that, I just might end up in jail."

"I won't kid you, Kitty. The D.A. would love to pin a murder case on you. But there are some loose ends. Like the fact that you have no apparent motive. And this Barbados nut appears not to be so easy to come by as well. Somebody went to a lot of trouble to kill Rich Evan or his dog. Either way, we're checking every lead out."

"Fang Danson claims Mr. Evan called him on the morning of his death and Mr. Evan boasted he had gotten lucky with someone the night he died."

"Good for him."

She ignored this TMR—typical male response. "Have you

tried to track the woman down? She could be an important witness."

"You are kidding, right? What's the D.A. going to do? Take out an ad in the L.A. Times." He held up his hands. "Anyone having slept with Rich Evan before he died, please contact your local law enforcement agency." The detective laughed. "Imagine how many calls we'd get?"

"It's better than doing nothing."

"No," he said firmly, "you do like I said. Keep out of this. Take care of your pets. Cook your heart out. We'll get to the bottom of things." He checked over the bill and laid some money on the table. "How about a movie?"

"I can't." Kitty glanced at her watch. "I have to prep for next week's meals."

"Oh, sure. I understand." He stayed close to her all the way to her car.

"Thank you for lunch, Jack," Kitty said. She looked pointedly at the detective's hand which clung to her door like it had nowhere else to go. "Is there something else?"

His feet pawed the sidewalk. "You never did say where you went last night—after you left Mrs. Randall's, that is."

Kitty's jaw dropped. She tried counting to ten, but it did no good. The pressure inside her only grew.

She grabbed the door and pulled it out of his grip. It slammed against her knee. She'd probably given herself a humdinger of a bruise. Be limping for the next three days. "I went to see a friend. Her name is Velma Humphries. She works at a Jack-In-The-Box in Culver City." She spat out the intersection and tossed in Velma's home phone number for good measure.

"Then we went to a pet store in West L.A." She was purple with rage—as mad at herself for being taken in by his charm and boyish good looks as she was at him for being such a conniving jerk.

"I bought a bird. For a client. Then we went to dinner on the boardwalk. Me, Velma and the bird." She spat out its name before he could ask for it. "You want to know what I ate?" She wasn't waiting for an answer. "Then I went home. To sleep. Alone."

Kitty fired up the car and sped off. He could have given her a traffic ticket for that. That and the expired parking meter. Yet he whistled all the way to his Jeep, a smile on his face.

Oh, sure. She was high strung and high maintenance. But all God's creatures were as special as they were unique.

And Libby liked her. And Lib's intuition was keen when it came to judging people. If Lib had been human herself, she'd have made a hell of a cop.

# 22

"Consuelo?"

The kitchen door was ajar and Kitty pushed it open with her toe. Images of Rich Evan lying face down in Benny's dog food jumped into her mind and she chased them away.

Mrs. Randall had warned Kitty. In fact, the last time Kitty had spoken with Mrs. Randall, the woman had made her promise not to step foot in the Wright house again. And she was about to do just that now. She had to. Rich Evan had died here and there must be some clue to his death to be found. And despite what Jack Young said, she was going to find it.

She glanced over her shoulder looking for the neighbor, Florence Goodman, but there was no sight of her. A big black Mercedes sat in the Goodman drive though. So someone was probably home.

But where was Consuelo? The kitchen was quiet and empty. "Consuelo?" whispered Kitty. This was too creepy. One by one, she pulled open the kitchen cabinets looking for Barbados nut, not that she even knew what it would look like if she stumbled on it. She checked the spice rack hoping to find a jar clearly labeled, but no luck.

She slowly walked into the media room. It was deserted. Down the hall she saw the draperies flapping. Someone had left one of the sliding doors open.

Was Consuelo on the deck? Kitty checked. The deck was unoccupied. A couple of bathers braved the cold Pacific, nothing more.

Kitty went to Mr. Evan's room. The master suite was in the far corner of the ground floor with an ocean view. The door was open. The room was empty as a mausoleum. The massive platform bed was unmade. The curtains were closed and the ocean was hidden.

On impulse, Kitty went to the night table on the rumpled side of the bed and pulled open the top drawer. A box of tissue, a platinum lighter and other paraphernalia filled the drawer halfway. A black leather address book tossed amongst a clutter of CDs, a third of them Beach Boys recordings, and magazines caught her eye.

The phone rang and she jumped. Kitty stuffed the address book in her purse and held her breath. After several more rings, the call stopped. Kitty wondered if the caller had given up or whether a machine had picked up the phone. Or was someone in the house with her? And had they answered the phone?

A lodestone of evil, Mrs. Goodman had said. One blew

his brains out, another was poisoned, one spontaneously combusted. . .

Kitty found herself running from the room. She stopped near the front door. A faint smell seemed to drift down from upstairs. What was it?

She crept to the stairway and inhaled. Sandalwood? Slowly she climbed the steps as if pulled there by an invisible string. A door at the top of the stairway was ajar mere inches. The brass doorknob was frigid as an ice block and the door opened with a creak.

The room was darkly shaded and lit only by a half dozen candles atop the dresser on the wall to Kitty's right. Images of skeletons lined the walls. More images, some carved of wood, some made of mosaics of bright shiny tiles, filled the small bedroom. The incense came from a brazier atop a small blackened altar. Gray smoke slowly wafted upward. A replica of Christ on the cross hung directly across the room. A single bed was on the wall opposite the dresser and mirror. Its bedspread was blood red with black pillows. The walls and ceiling were maroon.

A red-framed picture hung over the bed. It depicted a wedding couple. The man was in a gray suit with a red bow-tie and black sombrero. The woman wore a traditional white gown and clutched a bouquet of roses. Both had grinning skeleton heads.

Behind the door, a brightly painted life-size skull was crawling with equally bright acrylic caterpillars and lizards. It made Kitty's skin crawl and she backed up. She had to get out of this room.

A sharp, hard claw came down on Kitty's shoulder. She

screamed and spun.

"What are you doing in here?"

Kitty gasped. "Consuelo!"

Consuelo's hands were on her hips and she thrust her chest forward. "What are you doing here?" she demanded again. "Have you come to spy on me?"

"N–no." Kitty shook head firmly. "It's nothing like that. Really."

Consuelo's jaw worked back and forth like she was grinding corn into meal.

"I was in the neighborhood and only wanted to check in on you."

Consuelo's eyes were flat and narrow.

"I'm on my way to Angela Evan's house."

"You are wondering about my room, aren't you?" Consuelo moved closer to Kitty, forcing her further into the room.

"No, I wasn't. I called your name and there was no answer. I smelled your incense burning—it's really quite lovely, sandalwood, isn't it? And, anyway, I came up to investigate. I mean, to see if you were up here."

"Much of this is Mexican folk art designed for *El Dia de los Muertes*. You are familiar with this?"

Kitty gulped. "The Day of the Dead, right?"

"That's correct. We honor our dead and celebrate the continuity of Life."

"Is that today?" Kitty forced her lips into something resembling a friendly smile.

Consuelo shook her slowly head. "No. But living in this house. . .one must fight the evil spirits."

Did Consuelo consider Rich Evan one of the evil spirits? "About that," began Kitty, "if I could only ask you what you know. I mean, you lived here with Mr. Evan. Did you ever see or hear anything unusual, Consuelo?"

"I have already told you all that I know." Consuelo marched to the door and pointed. "You must leave now."

Kitty nodded. She wanted out of Consuelo's bedroom more than anything and breathed deep once she was safely out in the hall. Still, she stayed away from the balustrade and kept her back to the wall. The more she uncovered about Consuelo's personal side, the less safe Kitty felt around her.

Kitty followed Consuelo down the stairs. "So what will happen to you now, Consuelo?"

"Rich Evan promised me fifty-thousand dollars in his will. His lawyers say there is no such instruction." She spat. "Another of his lies, just like the lie of helping my father and my younger brother."

Kitty made appropriate sounds of sympathy. But inside she was thinking this was a motive for murder.

"I have been told by the lawyers that I can stay in the house until it is sold. They say they are being generous with me." Again, she spat. "Then. . ." She shrugged.

"I'm sure you'll find another position. I'll bet Angela Evan will give you a good reference."

Consuelo snorted.

"You and Mrs. Evan didn't get along?"

"About as well as her and Mr. Evan did."

"How about Mr. Evan's last wife, Tracy? Did you know Tracy Taylor?"

"Yes, I knew her."

"Had she been around recently? Have you seen her since the divorce, Consuelo?"

Again, Consuelo shrugged. "She's come by a time or two. Brought that dog, didn't she?"

Kitty nodded. "Was Tracy here the day Rich Evan died?"

"You'd have to ask her that, now wouldn't you?" Consuelo opened the front door. "The real estate company is bringing a client by soon and I have cleaning to do. Besides, they won't like it if you're here. The agents are fussy when they're showing their fancy million dollar homes to millionaires. Millionaires are fussy, too."

Kitty paused on the steps. The warm sun hit her back. "I still don't understand where Benny was the morning poor Mr. Evan died. That poison might have been meant for him."

"That dog was always running around everywhere. He only got himself locked out. Lucky for him." A hint of a grin formed along Consuelo's lips. "Unlucky for Mr. Evan."

Yes, thought Kitty. Unlucky, indeed. "Suppose someone wanted to poison Benny out of spite because they were angry with Mr. Evan or were trying to frighten him or warn him off. Don't you suppose that might be possible?"

"Like me, you mean?"

"No, of course not, I didn't mean—" Of course, this was exactly what Kitty had meant.

But the housekeeper cut her off. "My English may not be so great, but I know exactly what you mean, Miss Karlyle. You are accusing me of murdering Mr. Evan."

"Did you?"

Consuelo's eyebrow lifted and her eyes danced like they were on fire. "Now why would I do that?"

Why, indeed?

# 23

Bird in hand, Kitty once again pressed the buzzer, announcing her presence at Angela Evan's home.

"I sure hope she likes you," Kitty said, sticking her finger through the bars of the cage and stroking the cockatiel's wing feathers. The cage was growing heavy in her arm. The same arm was holding the bag from the pet shop that contained the bird book, food and all the other cockatiel-related merchandise she'd picked up for Angela.

She sighed and transferred this bag to her free hand and tapped her foot. Kitty pressed the buzzer again and stepped back. "What have I gotten you into?" Kitty asked the bird. He flapped his wings in reply.

"I'm going to have to set you down." Kitty bent and was in the process of lowering the cage to a shady corner of the porch when she heard the crash.

Kitty screamed and the cage dropped from her hands. The cockatiel screamed angrily as the cage rolled down the steps and came to a stop against a huge red clay pot that now marked the spot where she'd been standing only a moment earlier. The planter was busted into a hundred pieces, some large and some small. One shard had struck her in the leg. But she had her slacks on and no damage had been done. Gallons of black dirt covered the sidewalk and porch.

The front door was thrown open and Angela Evan herself, wrapped in a pink terrycloth robe ran out. "My goodness? Are you okay?" She ran to Kitty's side and laid a hand on her shoulder.

She looked up at the ledge where Kitty now saw a matching companion to the broken pot still stood. "That oaf, Gil," Angela complained, "I told him to water the plants not throw them off the balcony." She took Kitty by the arm and led her into the foyer. "I am so sorry, dear. Not hurt, are you?"

Kitty shook her head. She was trembling. She could have been killed! "The-the bird." Kitty pointed out the open door. The cage was tipped on its side and the bird was hopping madly about.

"Of course. Don't worry. Your bird looks all right."

A door that Kitty hadn't really noticed before slid open. It was an elevator and Gil Major stepped out of it. He wore an immaculate dark suit and white shirt. "I am sorry, Mrs. Evan. I was only intending to check the foliage, for parasites, and," he heaved his shoulders, "I'm afraid the planter got away from me."

"Please be more careful in the future, Gil. Someone might

get hurt."

He nodded.

"After you've brought in Miss Karlyle's things, clean up the mess you've made."

He nodded once again, this time bending his back even lower. Gil hurried out the door, carefully picked up the bird and the bag and brought them inside to the living room where Angela and Kitty now stood. He quickly departed.

Angela looked at the bird in the cage. Gil had set it on the coffee table in front of the chenille sofa. "What kind is it?"

"He's an Australian cockatiel." The cage was scratched and dented but the bird looked okay.

"I see."

"I've brought you a book on cockatiel care and some food and—"

"Yes, yes, yes," Angela said with a wave of her hand. "I'll give them to the housekeeper."

"Excuse me for asking, Mrs. Evan, but is Gil Major working for you now? Last time I was here, I remember seeing a young red-headed girl."

"Yes, I've taken Gil on. Giselle is incapable of taking care of everything around here."

"You let her go?"

"Heavens no. She's been with me ages. I simply brought in Gil to take care of the things she can't handle—the heavy stuff."

Like dropping giant pots on people's heads, wondered Kitty? And how did Gil Major go from working for the Randalls one day to Angela Evan practically the next?

"I fed him this morning. Oh, and here's your change."

Kitty rummaged through her purse and brought out a handful of paper bills and coins.

"Thank you. Now if you don't mind, I was about to take my sauna." Angela drew her robe up around her throat.

"Certainly. Would you like me to come back this evening and serve dinner?"

"To the bird?"

Kitty nodded.

"That would be fine. I may not be home, but I'll leave instructions that you are welcome anytime."

"Thank you." Kitty practically ran for the door.

"Does he have a name?" Angela asked.

"Who?"

Angela motioned towards the flapping bird. "This."

"The bird? No," Kitty replied somewhat slowly. "I thought you would like to name him yourself."

"Oh, of course." Angela thought a moment, then grinned. "I believe I shall name him Rich, Little Rich, in honor of my dear, departed husband. What do you think, Kitty?"

"Um, that's lovely," agreed Kitty, willing her eyes not to roll around in her skull.

She ran into Gil Major on the sidewalk, stooped over with a short-handled broom and dustpan, briskly cleaning up the near fatal mess. "Hello, Gil."

He swivelled and glanced up at her. "Miss Karlyle."

"What a surprise seeing you here." Kitty accidently stepped on triangle of broken pottery. It scrunched under her foot. "It's a shame about Mrs. Randall, isn't it?"

He set down his whiskbroom and straightened up. "Yes. Quite."

"I was at the Randall house the evening she died, feeding Mr. Cookie. She told me you were off for the evening."

He watched her but made no reply.

"And now she's dead and you're working for Angela Evan."

"Yes, funny thing, that, isn't it?" He looked at his dirty fingers and frowned.

Kitty nodded. "How do you know Mrs. Evan?"

"I didn't know Mrs. Evan. I know Giselle. We'd once worked for the same hotel. She'd been telling me that Angela Evan was looking to increase her household staff and with Mrs. Randall gone, I didn't know if Mr. Randall would be keeping me on. . ."

"So you switched employers."

"Precisely." He resumed his work. "Now, if you don't mind. I'd best clean up this mess."

"Of course." She watched him a moment, his wrist flicking rhythmically back and forth, whiskbroom in hand. "Mr. Cookie is coming back to health nicely."

"Wonderful."

"I can't imagine how he'd been poisoned. Dr. Landau, the vet, says it was definitely this Barbados nut thing again."

"Perhaps you had best check your ingredients more carefully. It seems to me you've caused quite enough harm, Miss Kitty."

"And then poor Mrs. Randall," Kitty ignored his shot and shook her head. "Strangled to death in her own home. I wonder who would do such a thing? Mrs. Randall was a harmless, dear woman."

"We mustn't speak ill of the dead, eh?"

"What do you mean?"

"Come off it," he said, a touch of harshness creeping into his tone, "we both know she was an overbearing, prissy, domineering woman who never had a kind word for anyone but her precious Mr. Cookie."

Interesting. Except for the bit about Mr. Cookie, that description sounded awfully apt for Angela Evan as well. "Who do you think killed her?"

He tossed a dustpan full of potting soil into the shrubbery. "I really wouldn't know. I'm a houseman not a detective. Perhaps it was that spiritualist of hers."

"Madame Zouzou? Maybe, but why?"

"Who knows?" He dusted himself off and strode to the door. "Maybe a ghost told her to do it."

Kitty's eyes widened. "Do you believe in ghosts, Gil?"

Gil Major's eyes locked in on hers as if framing an enigma between the two of them. "I believe the dead should stay dead, Miss Karlyle." He pulled the door handle. "If you do see a ghost, perhaps he, or she," the houseman added, "fervently wishes to live." He showed his teeth. "And these spirits will do anything for a chance to rejoin the living."

"Anything?"

He nodded. "Even if it means taking the life of another."

Goose bumps crawled over Kitty's flesh and she felt as if one of the Living Dead was rubbing up against her skin. The last thing Kitty saw before Gil closed the door in her face was his sharp-toothed smile. It blinked like a nefarious and incorporeal spirit then disappeared.

# 24

Richard and Timothy, Hollywood's self-proclaimed "gayest couple" were throwing a party. And it was a big one. Kitty had to plead with the valet not to take her car but rather help her get past the fifty-thousand dollar and up vehicles clogging the drive.

Feed the dogs, Us and Them, and the cockatiel and get out, that's all Kitty wanted to do. Loud music and a bass so pounding that it felt like an unstoppable earthquake resounded through the canyon.

A bustling kitchen welcomed her. Kitty managed to stop one of the hurrying party helpers long enough to ask where the dogs were. He only shrugged and said, "Beats me. I'm just a temp."

Kitty sighed and set down her trays. Dinner was getting cold. The kitchen door swung open revealing a party in full swing. There were hundreds in attendance and the party spilled out into the expansive backyard. Half the guests looked like they could have been celebrities. Kitty recognized many of their faces.

Kitty spotted Richard holding sway over a small crowd near the saltwater aquarium and shyly approached. He beamed when he saw her. "Kitty, my love! Good to see you!" He embraced her. "Come to join the party?"

She shook her head. "I've come to feed the dogs—and your bird. Where are they?"

"Ah," he nodded. "I've put them in the guest house. All these people," he waved his hands, "makes the babies a little nuts."

It's making me a little nuts, too, mused Kitty. "Okay, I'll take the food to them out back, if that's all right?"

"Of course, love. And afterward, come back and join the party." He was practically shouting over the music and the conversation to make himself heard.

"I'd love to, but I have one more client to serve this evening."

"So, come back after you've finished. Believe me," he said with a half-drunk grin, "the party will still be going on no matter how late you arrive."

"Thank you," she uttered noncommitally. She dodged revelers left and right, scooped up the pets' dinners and headed out to the guest house. The music vibrated her ears and drummed into her skull. It was oddly familiar yet unfamiliar all at the same time.

The guest house was larger than the house Kitty had grown up in. It even had its own courtyard with a small swimming pool in the middle. The Dalmatians were happy to see her, or maybe they were simply starved. In any event, she unwrapped their dinners and watched them eat. The cockatiel pecked away at his food as well.

Kitty was cleaning up her things when she heard shouting. She peaked out the window. Fang Danson and Angela Evan were arguing. Angela's arms were flying. Fang's were, too. Were they coming close to taking swings at each other?

Fang hollered some more, but his voice was muffled and Kitty couldn't make out a single word. A moment later, the tall man stomped off.

Kitty grabbed her trays and, on impulse, hurried after him. She lost him on the dark grounds, then caught sight of him again as he reappeared near the six-car garage to the left of the estate. Over her shoulder, Kitty saw that Angela had rejoined the party.

The rumble of an automobile drew her attention. A blue Aston Martin spun out of the garage and along the edge of the long drive, heading towards the street at a high speed. Fang Danson was at the wheel.

So much for him. Kitty decided to see what Angela Evan was up to. She tossed her trays in the Volvo and went back through the kitchen. A red-head at the sink, rinsing champagne glasses, caught her eye. "Excuse me," said Kitty, "but aren't you Giselle?"

The woman turned and smiled. Her hands were dripping with soapy water. "That's right."

"I'm Kitty Karlyle. Remember, I saw you out at Mrs. Evan's house yesterday."

"Oh, sure, I remember. You're the girl she's hired to cook for that bird of hers."

"That's right. I'm on my way over there now, in fact. Though if no one is home, I don't know how I'll get in. . ."

"Don't worry. Gil's there."

"That's right, Gil. He works there now. I almost forgot." She'd forgotten no such thing. "It must be nice for you, to have some help around that big house, I mean."

Giselle nodded.

"Especially since you two were already acquainted."

"Already acquainted?"

"Yes, I heard that you and Gil knew one another before he came to work for Mrs. Evan."

Giselle was shaking her head. "Whoever told you that is confused. I'd never met the man before." She looked around the room and lowered her voice. "If you want to know the truth, that man gives me the willies. I'm glad to get out of the house for a few hours. Making a few extra dollars working this here party is a lot nicer than being stuck in that house with Gil Major."

"Doesn't Mrs. Evan mind you moonlighting?"

"Nah. This was her idea. The gentlemen that live here mentioned they were short-handed on staff this evening and Mrs. Evan asked if I'd like to make some extra money."

"That was certainly kind of her." Kitty wondered if she was going to have to revise her opinion of Angela Evan upwards.

A tall woman with a high forehead and a sharp nose wearing a black wool blazer and matching skirt clapped her hands. "We have guests waiting for those in the billiards room," she said sharply.

Giselle snatched up a towel and quickly began drying the glasses. "Gotta go!"

Speaking of which, Kitty suddenly remembered she was supposed to drive back out to Malibu to give Little Rich, Angela's cockatiel, his dinner. And a late dinner it was going to be. But the idea of going back to that house and being alone with Gil Major after he had practically killed her, intentionally or otherwise, creeped her out.

Did she dare call Velma and ask her to meet her out in Malibu just so she could feed a bird? Velma, friend that she was, would probably do it, too. It would be a terrific imposition, though.

However, did she dare go there alone? At night? With only Gil Major in the house?

Kitty stepped out of the noisy kitchen and dialed Velma's number. "What are you up to?"

"Nothing much. Surfing."

It took Kitty a minute to figure out what Velma meant. The only surfing Velma did was on the Web. "I know it's a huge imposition, but do you want to come out to Malibu with me?"

"What?"

Kitty explained her situation and uneasiness.

"Wow. Look, I wish I could, but I'm working the late shift tonight. Glen, the manager, has really been getting on my case. If I take off again, he might fire me and I haven't got that new job locked up yet."

"Oh," Kitty couldn't hide her disappointment. "Don't worry. It was silly of me to ask anyway."

"It wasn't silly at all. And if you get in trouble, you give me a call, okay?"

Kitty promised.

Arriving at Angela Evan's house in the Malibu Colony, Kitty couldn't help but look up at that ledge where the pot had come crashing down from.

Gil Major let her in and stepped aside to let her pass with the small tray she carried. "Little Rich is in the den."

Kitty tried to make small talk. "So, do you miss England, Gil?"

"What makes you think I'm English?" he barked.

Kitty quickly placed Little Rich's food bowl inside the cage and shut the door. "I'm sorry," she gulped. "Am I wrong? I mean, your accent—"

He eyed her levelly. "What time will you be returning tomorrow?"

"Um, ten-thirty?" She backed away from the table. Why was she letting this guy get the best of her?

"Fine. Mrs. Evan would like it very much if you could keep to a tight schedule. She is an exacting woman."

"Yes, of course. I saw her tonight at a party that Richard Couric and Timothy Toms were hosting at their house."

Gil headed towards the front door in long, determined steps. Kitty followed. "She was arguing with Fang Danson."

Gil Major pulled open the door. "Goodnight, Miss Karlyle."

Kitty held her tongue and climbed in her car. Gil Major was a major pain.

Kitty woke early the next morning to get the most out of the day. Life had become too hectic. And her clients were spread out all across Southern California. Her job and the murders were taking a toll on her.

Kitty was determined to do nothing but cook today. Cook and take care of her clients' pets. Maybe she would forget all about trying to figure out why Rich Evan died and who killed Mrs. Randall—forget about haunted houses and the sordid lives of her clients.

Showered, dressed and bolstered by two cups of freshly ground coffee, Kitty got busy. She felt badly about ignoring her own pets, Fred and Barney, and gave them extra generous breakfast and rewarded Fred with a long walk around the block.

The telephone was ringing as she turned the key in the lock and she rushed to answer. "Hello?" she said breathlessly.

"Good morning. Man, I must have let the phone ring twenty times. You're a late sleeper."

Kitty's bubble of bliss burst. "You." Her lips scrunched up like she was sucking up the world's tartest lemon. "What do you want?"

"Oh, a third date would be nice," he drawled.

"A third—" It was all she could do to keep from slamming down the receiver. "We *never* had a second date." Her voice rose with each word and then each syllable. "We never had a *first* date."

"Hey, is that any way to talk to your fiancé?"

"You are not my fiancé."

"I asked you to marry me. You never said no." He chuckled over the line. "I take that for a yes."

"Well, then take this for a no. N–O. No!"

"You need more time. I can understand that."

"Is this the only reason you're calling this morning. Don't you have anything else to do with your life? Like open a can of Alpo, maybe?"

The detective allowed a short silence to pass and then said, "Actually, I did have some news."

"What? About our honeymoon?" quipped Kitty.

"See? Now you're getting it."

Kitty growled.

"Relax," said Young. "This is news you'll be interested in."

"Is it good news? Because if it's bad news, I'm not interested and I am hanging up."

"Hold on, hold on. Let me tell you and you can decide whether it's good or bad."

"I'm listening."

"Fang Danson was taken into custody late last night, or should I say, early this morning."

"What?" Had he killed Rich Evan? Was the nightmare over?

"That's right. He tried to run Angela Evan down with his car."

Kitty gasped. "Is she all right?"

"Oh, yeah. Everybody's fine. The two of them were having a big blow-up outside her house in the Colony. A neighbor called the L.A.S.D. after watching Fang go for Angela with his Aston."

Kitty chewed her lip. This wasn't good news or bad news. This was just weird news. "Do you think this has anything to do with Rich Evan's death, Jack? Or even Mrs. Randall's?"

"Who knows? Too early to tell. And Fang Danson and Angela Evan aren't talking. In fact, we already had to let Fang go."

"What?"

"That's right. The victim has refused to press charges. Mrs. Evan claims it was all a misunderstanding—Fang only lost control of his vehicle. If you ask me, he's lost control of his mind. Her, too. She was there when we let him out and they took off together, the happy couple and their lawyer."

Kitty had to think. Fang Danson tries to kill Angela Evan. Why? "I saw them last night, you know. At a party at a client's house. I saw Fang Danson and Angela Evan arguing there."

"Interesting," said Young. "What client is this?"

"Richard Couric and Timothy Toms. They have a house out in Benedict Canyon."

"I know where their house is." Was that an undertone of alarm she heard in his voice. "Those guys are clients of yours?"

Kitty said yes.

"I don't like it," said Young. "You should stay away from those two."

"What do you mean 'stay away from those two'? They're sweethearts. With two lovely dogs that they simply dote over and a cockatiel that they treat the same."

"Drop them."

"Drop them?! Are you mad? Richard and Timothy are two of my best clients. What's going on? What do you know about them and why don't you like them?"

"Nothing," he sighed. "Promise me you'll be careful, Kitty."

# 25

Mr. Randall sat in the study, rumpled and pale. His thin hair was pulled to one side. A dark blanket covered him. His body was a wrinkled mass of wool.

Kitty had brought Mr. Cookie a delicious four-course meal and he'd eaten every bit. The Randalls' regular cook, Patti Belle, had let her in and told her that Mr. Randall was locked away in the study.

Kitty had opened the door and was looking at him now. This was the same room that Mrs. Randall had been found dead in. Why was he sitting here now?

"Mr. Randall?"

His chin rested on his chest. Only his eyes lifted. "Miss Karlyle."

"How are you, sir?"

His answering shrug was barely perceptible.

"I brought Mr. Cookie his meal." She stepped a little further into the study. "Is there anything I can do for you?"

He shook his head. "No, dear."

"I'm very sorry about your wife. I'm sure they'll find whoever did this terrible thing soon." She waited, but he said nothing. "Well, I suppose I'd better be going."

His voice shot out. "So many people dying."

She turned. "Sir?"

"Mr. Evan, now Lucille. I never thought I'd face so much death. At my age, it is I who should be in the ground."

"Did you know Rich Evan well?"

"No." Mr. Randall rubbed his wrists. "Not well. He gave us permission to use one of his tunes for a commercial for our stores. And we played golf a time or two. A fine young man, sorry to see him go."

"Yes, sir. Have the police questioned the psychic, Madame Zouzou, about Mrs. Randall's death?"

He snorted derisively. "Psychic! Ah, my wife and her indulgences. Always trying to help others. She liked to meddle, she did. Bless her heart." Mr. Randall crossed his legs and grimaced. "The police went to the home of Madame Zouzou. She lives in Tarzana. But she was not there. Her roommate says Madame left for Sedona, Arizona, the day after my wife's death. On her way to some sort of crystal skulls conference—whatever that is."

"I see."

"They are trying to track her down now. They have spoken to my wife's friends. Those who were at the seance. No one noticed anything unusual and the seance was over by midnight."

He came unsteadily to his feet and took Kitty's hands. His fingers were icy. "You will keep cooking for Mr. Cookie, won't you? Mrs. Randall would want that. After all, she has always had a soft spot for Mrs. Humphries."

"Yes, Mr. Randall. I'd be happy to."

He smiled and patted her hand. "Good. Too many changes around here. I don't like changes." His eyes teared up.

"I heard about Gil Major leaving."

"Ummm, just as well. He was an odd bird."

Kitty couldn't agree more. "Had he been with you long, sir?"

"Six months or so."

."Do you mind if I ask how he came to be employed by you?"

He rubbed his unshaven jowls. "Well, that's Lucille's department. I left all the household matters to her. But, as I recollect, he was referred to her. Same as you."

Kitty heard a phone ringing in the distance. Patti Belle appeared and told Mr. Randall that the office was calling. He told her to tell them to go away.

He picked up a silver picture frame holding a shot of his wife in younger days. "We were married fifty-three years in January." Mr. Randall seemed to disappear into the photo and Kitty decided to leave him there.

But he stopped her. His words came out strong. "My wife always meant well."

"Sir?"

He sagged and laid the picture down on the table. "She always meant well."

"She was always kind to me," replied Kitty.

"How is Mrs. Humphries' granddaughter? Velma, isn't it?"

"Yes, it's Velma."

"A good girl, is she?"

Kitty smiled. "The best, Mr. Randall."

He seemed delighted. "How's she doing?"

Kitty explained how she'd been having some trouble since finishing culinary school but how things were now looking up with a shot at a chef's position at one of L.A.'s best restaurants.

"I look forward to eating there. And you tell her she should come visit me sometime. Not to be a stranger. We're practically family, after all."

"I'm sure she'll be happy to hear that. And again, I want to express my condolences on your wife," Kitty said softly. "I had spoken to her just Saturday evening."

He sighed mournfully. "And I was out of town on business. Sometimes, I believe I've spent too much time building up this business and too little with family and friends. Tell me, did Lucille seem happy when you saw her?"

Kitty decided to be tactful. "Yes, sir. She was looking forward to the seance."

Mr. Randall nodded. He seemed to find solace in this simple statement.

"To be honest, she did get a little shaken when I asked her about the Wright house."

Mr. Randall blanched. "Did you say the Wright house?"

Kitty nodded.

"Oh, dear."

"Rich Evan owned the Wright house at the time of his death, you see. Didn't you know?"

Mr. Randall shook his head and tumbled back into his chair. His hands clutched the bolsters.

"Your wife said that you knew someone who'd lived there previously—a Bruce Churchill? He was an attorney." Mr. Randall's eyes stared listlessly at the distant wall. "Mr. Randall? Are you all right?"

"Bruce Churchill was a fine young man. And a promising attorney." He groaned and pressed his face into his hands. "But that was long, long ago."

Kitty had a sudden inspiration. "What ever happened to his lover?" Could it have been a young Lucille Randall? That would explain her strong reaction to hearing the name from the past suddenly brought back to haunt her. "Do you remember his lover's name?"

There was a long pause before he answered and that was only to say, "I do not remember."

"Are you sure? Think, Mr. Randall. This could be important. I mean, what if your wife's death and Mr. Evan's are somehow related?" Kitty knew this was grasping at straws but straws were practically all she had. And if there was a connection between Rich Evan and Lucille Randall, no matter how tenuous, she was determined to uncover it.

Had the Wright house's evil spread? Mrs. Randall had said that Madame Zouzou was going to attempt to contact some spirits that had inhabited the Randall house previously. Did this have something to do with her death?

Mr. Randall was shaking his head. "I don't see how this is possible, Miss Karlyle. It was all so long ago."

"We all make mistakes, Mr. Randall. I'm sure your wife—"

He eyed Kitty with sad amusement. "You think it was Lucille?" Mr. Randall shook his head. "No."

Kitty realized she'd stepped way over the line. "I apologize. I didn't mean to imply anything, Mr. Randall, sir."

"Bruce's lover was declared insane. Landed in an asylum. Here in L.A." He swivelled his head. "That's all I can tell you. I made a promise. Do you understand?"

Kitty nodded.

"Oh, maybe it doesn't matter any longer." His lifeless eyes stared straight ahead. "Everyone is dead now. Kresge," he said at a near whisper. "It was Kresge."

Kitty longed to ask more but old Mr. Randall was too far gone. She'd better tell Patti Belle to come take care of him.

Head in hands, Mr. Randall uttered, "Lucille always meant well."

# 26

Was the Randall house haunted, too? Kitty wondered. Was it cursed? These thoughts played through her mind and preyed on her sanity as she swept through L.A. Her last stop was going to be the Rabinowitz's.

Mr. and Mrs. Rabinowitz were dining while listening to a lively CD that seemed a bit out of character for the normally subdued couple. In the track running as Kitty laid out Goldie's dinner (a selection of California vegetables bought at the Farmers Market and fresh tuna), the guy was singing some goofy tune about somebody named Cow Patti.

"Interesting," she remarked as Mr. Rabinowitz caught her eye and grinned. Kitty laid out Goldie's menu card.

*Kitty Karlyle Gourmet Pet Chef*

—*California Goldie Rush*—

*1 cup tuna, lightly browned*
*½ cup crushed baby carrots*
*½ cup finely chopped green beans*
*1 cup risotto, steamed*
*pinch kosher salt*
*pinch basil*
*1 tsp. olive oil*

"It's Jim Stafford."

Mrs. Rabinowitz was nodding. "We saw his show in Branson, Missouri, when we drove out there two months ago. Funniest thing you ever saw."

"Mr. Rabinowitz just had to have one of Mr. Stafford's CDs. He sells them in his gift shop."

"We saw Andy Williams, too," Mr. Rabinowitz added as he chomped down on a huge square of cheese and spinach filled ravioli. "What a crooner."

Kitty left them humming along to a ditty about spiders and snakes. Her cellphone burst into song itself as she entered the mass of traffic on the Hollywood Freeway. It was Jack. "Not now," she said, "not again."

"Sorry, I can't seem to help myself."

"Well, I can. Goodbye, detective."

"Hold on. I've got news." He paused for effect. "And it concerns you."

Kitty dropped in behind a delivery truck in the center lane

and balanced the phone between her ear and shoulder. She really needed one of those hands-free thingies. "I'm listening."

"Tracy Taylor Evan has been arrested in the murder of her ex-husband, Rich Evan."

"What?" Kitty's eyes left the road and she'd crossed over. The driver she'd almost sideswiped was giving her the finger. She recovered and slowed. "Tracy Evan?"

"That's right."

"Why? How?"

"Why don't you come down to the station and I'll tell you all about it. I'm here now."

"I don't know." Did she really want to get further involved? Did any of this really matter? After all, Tracy Taylor Evan had been arrested and Kitty was off the hook. The best thing to do was to forget any of this happened.

Of course, there was still poor Lucille Randall. Her murderer was still out there someplace. But no doubt the police would find him or her soon enough. "No," she said finally, firmly. "I've had enough of this entire nasty business. I'm going home. To bed."

"She wants to talk to you."

"Who?" His voice was cutting in and out. There was some sort of disturbance with the cell service.

"Tracy. After the police picked her up she hollered and protested and beat the walls screaming she was innocent. Talked to a lawyer for fifteen minutes. Then he left. I don't think he could take the shouting any longer. That girl's got lungs."

"She's a singer."

"So I've heard. Anyway, after raving a bit she demanded that she speak to you. We haven't been able to get a thing out of her since. She says she's talking to you or nobody. So," Young said again, "how about it?"

"But why me?"

He chuckled. Through the static-filled lines it came out more of a monster-like gurgle. "Why don't you come down to the jail and find out?"

Kitty's curiosity got the best of her and she agreed. The detective gave Kitty directions and said to ask for him when she arrived.

Det. Young led Kitty back to a small office. "Have a seat."

Kitty took the small chair opposite the narrow desk.

"Can I get you anything? Coffee?"

"No, thanks. You said Tracy Taylor wanted to speak with me. Can I see her now?"

"Let me give you the background first."

Kitty nodded and folded her hands.

"It turns out Tracy Evan, Rich's ex, was in the Malibu Colony the day of his death. The mistake we made—" He looked up at Kitty. "Yes, we do make mistakes—was that when we checked the gatehouse log to see if Rich Evan had any visitors only your name showed up. It turns out as we dug deeper that Tracy Taylor Evan was also in the log."

"How could the police have missed that?"

"Easy. She was signed in to see a Yolanda Squires, a friend of hers from her days married to Rich Evan."

"I see. But I still don't see how that makes her a killer."

"It gets better. Tracy was seen outside her ex's house by a Mrs. Goodman. Now, the Squires home is at the opposite end of the colony."

"She got lost?" Good old Mrs. Goodman. Was there anything that woman didn't see?

"No." Young was smiling. "Tracy has already admitted going to the Evan house. In fact, she admitted to taking Benny. Said she was angry with Rich for not being more friendly towards her. Said she'd given him the dog and she figured she could just as easily take it back."

"So that's why Benny wasn't around when I brought him his food." Kitty shook her head with disbelief. "But why did Tracy bring Benny back?"

"She says she had a change of heart."

Kitty frowned and scrunched up her forehead.

Jack waved his finger. "It doesn't look good when you do that, you know."

"Do what?" The rows in her forehead went even deeper.

"That. Make that face."

She stuck out her tongue at him. "So she meant to kill Rich Evan? Is that what you're saying?"

"I'm not saying anything. Neither is she. Yet. Maybe she meant to take the dog. Maybe she meant to kill him. Maybe she got Benny out of the way, locked up in her car, and talked Rich into eating the dish himself."

He stood. "Maybe she got him to eat it at gunpoint." He stepped into the hall and waved for Kitty to follow. "Why don't you ask her?"

# 27

Kitty did just that. She was led to a small interrogation room where Tracy Taylor Evan sat behind a long table in a too-large orange jumpsuit. A uniformed female guard stood behind her.

After a word between the officer and Det. Young, Kitty and Tracy were left alone.

"I didn't do it," Tracy said the minute the two cops were gone.

"Why should I believe you? And why are you telling me this, anyway?" Kitty paced. Being closed in made her nervous. "Shouldn't you be telling your attorney?"

Tracy shrugged. "I already told him. He says to give it a couple days. Says maybe I can make bail." Her eyes looked empty. "I don't have any money though."

"I'm sorry."

Tracy leaned forward. "Listen, I have to tell you. You have to understand. I am being framed." Her voice was a blend of fear and urgency. "You were framed, too."

"How am I being framed?" After all, Tracy was the one being arrested for murder.

"It was your food that this Barbados nut stuff was in, wasn't it?"

Kitty nodded. "You know about Barbados nut?" This could be all the police needed to nail the woman.

"I didn't know nothing about it until this murder. And I am not a killer. I don't think you are either."

"The police said there was a witness who could place you at Mr. Evan's house."

Tracy slammed her hands on the table. Kitty jumped. "I told them I went there. I confessed to it!" She fought to regain her composure. "I took Benny. I'd given Rich the puppy as a present—a gift. I was trying to be nice, you know?"

Kitty smiled. "So he'd be nice back to you?"

Tracy grinned. "Yeah," she admitted. "That's it."

"But Rich wasn't being nice, was he?"

"No, he wasn't. I was on my way to Yolanda's house. I'd known her from the time I was married to Rich. We're still friends. Anyway, I just figured I'd drive by the old house, you know?

"And what do I see when I do? I see Benny tied up on the side of the yard. And I just freaked, I guess. I got so angry that I stopped, snatched him up and drove off." Tracy shook her head. "I guess that's when that nosy neighbor lady saw me.

"Anyway, after driving around a little while, I realized what I'd done was stupid and that taking the dog wasn't going to make Rich treat me any better. So I took him back."

"Did you see Rich? Did you talk to him?"

"No, I didn't see or talk to anybody. I only opened up my car door and let Benny loose. He ran up to the house and I drove off."

"I see." Kitty sat across from the young woman.

"Yeah. And now the police are talking like I killed Rich and asking me whether I meant to kill him or the dog." Tracy's eyes were pleading. "I didn't kill anybody, Kitty."

"I still don't understand why you're telling me all this."

Tracy sighed. "Because it was your food that the poison was in. Somebody is framing you, too. Don't you get it? Fang and Angela, Richard and Timothy." She was biting her thumb.

"Richard Couric and Timothy Toms?"

"They're bad." She leaned closer. "They want to do bad things to you."

"Bad things?" Kitty smiled. Surely, Tracy was kidding. Or psychotic. "Why would any of the people you mention want to hurt me? I only feed their pets."

Tracy's eyes were hard and flat. "Because they are killers. They killed Rich and they need a scapegoat." Tracy reached out and grabbed Kitty's hand above the wrist. "They got me and they're going to try to get you, too."

Kitty pulled her arm free. "That's ridiculous." Images of that big pot falling off Angela's balcony exploded before her eyes. "Are you telling me that Fang Danson and Angela Evan and even Richard and Timothy are all in this together?"

Tracy tilted her head. "Why not? They're business partners. Rich, he was one of them, too." She raised an eyebrow. "Now he's dead. One less person to share the profits with."

"But why would they hurt me?" Kitty's face had lost its color.

"Like I said, they need the police to blame someone or someones. That's us. Besides, you've been snooping around. They don't like that."

The interrogation room door opened quietly, letting in a whoosh of cool air. The female officer told Kitty it was time for the prisoner to go.

"What about Lucille Randall?" Kitty said quickly. "Did they kill her, too?"

"Who? Randall? Never heard of her." A spark of recognition lit up her eyes. "Oh, that rich lady that got killed." Tracy shook her head. "I saw it in the papers. Yeah. But I don't know anything about her."

She motioned for Kitty to come closer and whispered in her ear. "You keep an eye on Angela and Fang. If anyone is behind all this, it's her. The bitch. And Fang, well, she's got him wrapped around her finger. You talk to him. See if he maybe lets something slip."

"But Fang was Rich's best friend. Surely, Fang wouldn't have anything to do with his murder."

"Fang hasn't had a hit in years. This CD he's working on means the world to him. It's make it or break it time, if you know what I mean. People get funny when it comes to money. And fame."

Kitty nodded. Tracy, having gone through the millions of

her settlement, would certainly know the truth of her own words. "How about Kresge?"

The guard lifted Tracy to her feet. "Time to go."

"Huh?"

"Have you ever heard of a woman named Kresge?"

Tracy shrugged as the officer led her away.

# 28

Det. Young took Kitty's arm and led her back to his office.

"What about Mrs. Randall?" Kitty asked, crossing her legs with a sigh. "Did Tracy Evan kill her too?"

"No," replied Jack. "She was working—waiting tables at a place in the Valley. All kinds of witnesses. It would have been impossible." He rested his chin on his elbows. "So what did she want to talk to you about, Kitty?"

Kitty thought a moment. Would it be fair for her to reveal what Tracy had said in private? Was she breaking some sort of trust? She supposed not. After all, Tracy hadn't asked her to keep any secrets and she certainly hadn't promised to do so. Kitty repeated much of what Tracy had told her.

"That's what she told us." The detective was spinning a pencil across his desktop.

"She thinks it's a setup. Tracy blames Fang Danson, Angela Evan and even Richard Couric and Timothy Toms for her predicament. She blames them for my troubles, too. What is it with Richard and Timothy, anyway? You warned me about them, as well. They're so sweet. What does everyone have against them?"

Jack glanced out his open door. The hall was empty. "I really shouldn't be telling you this." He leveled a finger at her. "So don't go repeating it. Technically, it's only hearsay."

"I haven't heard *anything* yet."

"Richard Couric and Timothy Toms are reported to be major league drug smugglers."

Kitty snorted. "You're joking! Those two guys? That's silly, Jack. They're harmless."

He shrugged. "Don't say I didn't warn you. We've been keeping an eye on them for a long time. But those guys are slick."

Kitty was shaking her head. "I still can't believe it."

"Believe it." Jack shuffled some papers around on his desk, found a fax he was looking for and scanned it before handing it to Kitty.

"What's this?"

"The police out in Sedona were finally able to track down that spiritualist, Madame Zouzou—what kind of name is that?—she's speaking at the Crystal Magic of the Skulls Conference at some inn out there. Anyway, according to the report we received, she doesn't know anything. Some psychic, huh?"

"Could this Madame Zouzou have murdered Mrs. Randall? That makes sense, doesn't it?"

"Yeah, that makes sense."

Kitty smiled.

"Except a friend of Mrs. Randall, one Winnie Lawford, gave Madame Zouzou a lift back to her house in Tarzana and Lucille Randall was very much alive at that time."

Kitty moaned. "Another dead end." No pun intended.

Jack nodded. "She did say something odd though."

"What's that?"

"According to Madame Zouzou, Mrs. Randall wanted her to try and contact some dead person named Kresge."

Kitty drew in a sharp breath. Her skin went clammy. Kresge. That name again.

"And she wanted to do it before her other guests arrived. Madame Zouzou says Mrs. Randall was quite distraught." He rolled his eyes. "Of course, she claims the cat was distraught, too."

"And did she?"

"Did she what?"

Kitty said evenly, "Did Madame Zouzou contact this dead person, Kresge?" She counted her heartbeats as she waited for Jack to respond.

"Yeah. She says she did, anyway. If you can believe her. She claims he was rocking the table and rattling the walls—spouting all kinds of bad mojo."

"Wait a minute." Kitty stiffened.

"What?"

"You just said *he*."

"So?"

"Kresge is a *she*." Kitty explained to Jack how Miss Kresge had been Bruce Churchill's lover and how they'd once lived in the Wright house. "Churchill committed suicide and his lover went insane."

"That may be, but Madame Nutjob definitely said Kresge was a he."

"Which means that Bruce Churchill's lover had been a man!" exclaimed Kitty. Her skin tingled. Maybe they were finally getting somewhere! "And this was years and years ago. Two male lovers. That explains all the secrecy. Homosexuality wasn't considered socially acceptable back then, not like it is now."

Jack was nodding. "Could be. So where is this all leading us?"

Kitty frowned. Where was it all leading them? Bruce Churchill had a male lover who went mad. Churchill was dead. If Madame Zouzou had contacted Kresge, that meant he was dead as well. So there would be no way to talk to him. Not unless she wanted to go through Madame Zouzou.

And Kitty wasn't sure she wanted to go that far. "I can't help thinking that Kresge is somehow the key to this. What ever happened to him?"

Jack shuffled some more papers. "They locked him up in a psychiatric hospital in L.A. He died there a few years back. I was just going to head over and follow up on it. Want to come?"

Kitty shook her head. "No. My head's pounding. I've had all I can stand for one day. I think I'll go see Velma." She needed a friend to talk to—someone to unload her burden on. Velma wouldn't mind. And she was sharp. Maybe she'd find something in all this that Kitty and the police were missing.

Kitty looked at her watch. "Velma should be home by now."

# 29

Kitty fell into her car. She was about to dial Velma's number to let her know she was coming over when she noticed her voicemail icon flashing. She dialed in and got a message from Velma herself.

"Hi, this is Velma. Uh, I was hoping you were around. I can't find my watch. I think I might have taken it off at the sink at the house of those two guys, Richard and Timothy, when I went with you on your rounds that day. I like to take it off when I'm doing the dishes and we scrubbed out those dog bowls. . ." Pause. "I don't know their last names or their phone number, so I'm just going to swing by and see if they have my watch. If I can find the place, that is. Well, guess that's all. Call me if you get this message. . ."

Oh, no! Velma was on her way to Richard and Timothy's house. And according to Jack they were drug dealers, or worse yet, killers!

The car key rattled in Kitty's trembling hand. Velma's message was time-stamped over forty-five minutes ago. It wasn't far to Richard and Timothy's, and Velma was probably coming from Culver City.

Kitty shoved the key in the ignition. She just might make it.

As the engine grumbled to life, she decided to give Aunt Gloria a call. Maybe she had come up with something by now, too. She punched in her aunt's home number. "Hello, Aunt Gloria, how are you? It's me, Kitty."

Ignoring the fact that the place was full of police cars, Kitty sped through the parking lot looking for the exit out to the street. Velma didn't have a cellphone, but she'd call Velma's house anyway as soon as she got done speaking to her aunt.

Aunt Gloria's voice came through faint and crackly. "Kitty, I'm glad you called—" The phone hissed. "I left a message for you on your message machine at home. . ."

Kitty's cellphone beeped. The battery was running low and the reception stunk. "What?" She pressed her ear to the receiver.

"I did some digging around on the Wright house and on the Barbados nut like you asked and—"

Kitty cursed and banged the phone with the palm of her hand. "I'm sorry. All I'm getting is static!" she shouted. "And my battery is going dead. Aunt Gloria? Can you hear me?" Kitty cursed some more. "I'll charge up my phone and call you back when I get on the road."

She waited for a reply. "Aunt Gloria?" She looked at the

display. The connection was lost. Kitty whipped the car phone adapter out of the glovebox and hooked it up.

A trail of soft, low lights marked the long driveway to Richard and Timothy's estate. One of the dogs was barking. There was no sign of Velma's car.

Kitty took a slow, deep breath. Had they killed Velma and dumped the car and the body somewhere? The barking dog made her edgy. Overcoming her fear, she approached the side door.

Quiet Timothy, wearing brown spectacles, chinos and a black turtleneck sweater answered. "Kitty, what a surprise." He looked past her out to the drive. "You're alone?"

The back of Kitty's neck prickled. 'Are you alone?' That was an odd question, wasn't it?

"Come inside."

"Oh, ah, no, thanks." No way she was going inside, at night, alone, with no witnesses. Not after all the stories she'd heard. "I mean, I was wondering if my friend, Velma—you remember, she came and helped me feed Us and Them the other day?" Kitty rattled off a description. "Anyway, she said she might come by. She thought she might have left her watch here."

"Of course. Well," he said, letting his hand run down his chest, "we haven't seen your friend."

The dog was barking madly and Kitty turned her head trying to figure out where the sound was coming from.

"That's Us," said Timothy with a faint smile. "Probably sees a raccoon. Always makes him a little crazy. Are you sure you won't come inside?"

Kitty said no. "Besides, I-I have a friend waiting for me."

Timothy looked at her car. He seemed puzzled.

"He followed me over in his car. He's parked down at the street."

Timothy nodded. "I see. Well, goodnight then, Kitty. See you tomorrow."

"Goodnight, Timothy." Kitty raced back to her car. Blood was pounding in her ears as she made what she felt was her escape.

Racing through the hills, she tried Velma's home number. It rang and rang and rang.

Where was Velma? Had Timothy's dog been barking at a raccoon? Or was he barking at Velma? Or howling because Velma had been murdered. That did it, Kitty decided, if Velma wasn't home and wasn't at Jack-In-The-Box, she was calling the police.

Coming up the dark, narrow sidestreet, Kitty noticed that the lights were on at Velma's cottage out back of the Van de Wetering's 40's style ranch house, but it didn't look like the Van de Wetering's were home. Velma's car wasn't on the street but that didn't mean much. Sometimes she parked in the alley.

Kitty grabbed her phone—it held about a quarter-charge now—and stuck it in her pocketbook. Her footsteps made little sound on the narrow, snaking path leading to Velma's tiny cottage in the back yard. The night was cool and she regretted she hadn't brought a sweater to keep the chill out of her bones.

The sounds of an old B.A.D. Spike hit rattled the glass; a contemporary of M.C. Hammer, he'd made a splash, then disappeared. Kitty knocked on the door. The sound went off and the door opened a minute later.

"Hey, girl!" Velma smiled brightly. She still had on her Jack-In-The-Box uniform. She was wearing her watch. "What are you doing here?"

A flood of relief swept over Kitty like a six-foot ocean wave. After all the terrible things she had been imagining, it was good to see her friend again. Alive and well. "It's not too late is it? I'm not interrupting anything, am I?" Kitty glanced at the glowing computer screen on the corner of Velma's small desk.

"No, of course not. Come on in. What's wrong? You look terrible. Like you've just seen a ghost or something." Velma padded into the small square room and squatted on a pair of large pillows. A large bowl of some sort of tomato-based soup was nestled into the corner, giving off steam.

Velma didn't know how near the truth her words seemed. Kitty sat. The scent of food reminded her just how long it had been since she'd eaten.

Kitty pointed at her friend's arm. "You found your watch."

Velma rubbed her wrist. "Oh, yeah. Stupid me. I'd left it at work. I stopped at Jack-In-The-Box first, just in case, before heading out to see your clients. Glen had me cleaning pots and pans as penance for taking off the other day. Personally, I think he resents the fact that I'm a trained chef and he's not."

Kitty nodded. "Probably." Her stomach grumbled. Right about now, she'd settle for a sack full of cold Jack-In-The-Box leftovers.

"I'm just glad I got the watch back. Costs a bundle and it was a birthday present from Granny."

Velma must have noticed the look of hunger in her friend's eyes because she said, "Hungry?"

Kitty admitted she was. "But I'll eat later." She grabbed her stomach. "My stomach is so tied up in knots now, I'd be afraid to eat."

Velma carefully lifted her spoon to her lips and sipped. "Talk to me, Kitty. What's wrong?"

"I don't know where to even begin," said Kitty. She then proceeded to spill her guts, filling her bestfriend in on everything that had happened. Everything she had learned.

"Wow." Velma laid down her soup spoon and uncrossed her legs. "That's some tale. Spooks, spirits, poisonings, murders. . ."

"Tell me about it. Did you know that Mrs. Randall was into stuff like spiritualists?"

Velma shook her head. "I had no idea. Granny sure never mentioned it. Maybe this Zouzou person killed Mrs. Randall?"

"No, I already thought of that. It turns out that Madame Zouzou is at some Crystal Magic of the Skulls conference in Sedona. Whatever that is."

"Crystal skulls? Oh, sure," said Velma, "I've heard of them."

"You have?"

"Yeah, they're these skulls carved out of crystal that are supposed to contain supernatural powers or something. Some believers even claim they contain advanced alien knowledge left on Earth thousands of years ago. The trick is in trying to unlock the skulls to release the knowledge."

"I don't believe it."

"Believe it. There are a couple of people doing seminars who claim they are able to tap into the crystal skulls and communicate with these aliens and pass on their superior knowledge to us mere mortals."

Kitty looked dubious. "How do you know so much about crystal skulls?"

"It's all true. I read it in a mystery novel. You can learn a lot reading mysteries," Velma said sagely.

"I guess you're right. Anyway, this spiritualist, Madame Zouzou, says that Mrs. Randall asked her to try to contact this dead guy named Kresge before she died."

"That's weird. I wonder why?"

Kitty sighed. "We may never know."

"Tough. But at least you're in the clear from what you told me about this ex-wife of Rich Evan's being locked up."

"Yes," Kitty said, with a lack of conviction, "I suppose."

"So, how about that soup now?"

Kitty brightened. Already she felt more relaxed. It was nice to have someone to talk to besides pets all day. "I'd love some."

# 30

Detective Jack Young pulled into the parking lot of the Hollywood Hills Psychiatric Hospital, a dilapidated three-story stucco building tucked behind a couple of old highrises. Inside was another story. The walls were clean and white. The entrance brightly lit. He went to reception and asked to speak with someone about a former patient, Ken Kresge.

He was told to wait and wait he did for the better part of an hour before a comely nurse led him to a spacious office on the second floor where a bespectacled Ben Franklin looking man in a white jacket asked him to sit.

The man leaned forward. "Colin Bernhart." He held out his hand and the detective shook it before settling into a proffered chair. "I was told you wanted to ask me about a former patient of Hollywood Hills?"

"Yes, doctor. Ken Kresge." Young pulled out a small

notepad and pen. "Did you know him? Did you treat him?"

Dr. Bernhart folded his hands. "You know, detective, I really don't have to tell you anything. Patient confidentiality and all. But," he let the word hang there in the air a moment, like a threatening rain cloud, "I don't see what harm it could do. Mr. Kresge is deceased. I suppose his wife probably is by this time as well."

Det. Young stiffened. "Wife?"

"That's right. Mr. Kresge had been married."

"She came to visit him regularly?"

Dr. Bernhart shook his head. "Never. The way I understand it, they'd been estranged for years. Still, she must have cared for him."

"Why do you say that?"

"You see, the state paid for most all of Mr. Kresge's care here. But his wife used to send small sums of money from time to time. Small gifts also."

"I see. Do you have an address for this Mrs. Kresge, doctor?"

Dr. Bernhart pursed his lips. "I suppose we must have it on file here somewhere. I'll ask my assistant to run it down for you, if you like. I can't imagine what your interest in Mr. Kresge is. . ."

Jack smiled. "Just tying up some loose ends, doctor."

"I know that Mr. Kresge was involved in quite a sensational case many years ago. It's when he lost his mind. We never were able to do much for him over the years. He spoke little and interacted with no one."

Dr. Bernhart asked, "This couldn't possibly be connected with the old Churchill case, could it, detective? After all, that case is ancient history by now."

"How could it?" Jack replied. "Like you said, it's all ancient history. You don't believe in ghosts coming back and committing murders, do you, doctor?"

Dr. Bernhart's eyes twinkled. "I most certainly do not." He pressed the intercom on his desk. "Miss Banbury, would you please look up an address for Det. Young? That's right, a Mrs. Humphries."

Jack dropped his pen. "Did you say Humphries?"

"Yes. She'd been Kresge originally, of course," explained Bernhart, "but reverted to her maiden name after the incident."

"Thanks, doc!" Jack leapt from his chair and bolted out the door.

# 31

"I think I'll call Aunt Gloria. She was trying to reach me earlier—said she had some information."

"Sure," hollered Velma, making noises in the kitchen.

Kitty unclasped her purse and fished around for her phone. "Oh, look."

"What?" Velma's head appeared in the open doorway.

Kitty held a small black leather book in her fingers. "It's Rich Evan's phone book. I forgot I had this." She shook it.

Velma's eyes narrowed. "Where'd you get it?"

"I found it in Mr. Evan's bedroom." Kitty explained how she'd come upon it when she'd been snooping around at her employer's house.

"You always were a nosy one." Velma grabbed the little book, fell back onto her cushions and flipped through the pages. "Hmmm, interesting."

"What?"

"Ooops!" The book fell into Velma's soup bowl. "Darn!" Hot soup splashed all over Velma's uniform and soaked into the cushions.

"Quick, pull it out before it's ruined!" Kitty exclaimed.

"Don't worry, I'm sure I can save it. It'll be stained, but readable." Velma pulled herself up. "I'd better take this mess to the sink." Velma carefully carried the soup and address book off to the kitchen. "I'll clean this up and be right back."

"Can I help?"

"Nah, it's no big deal. Relax. I'll take care of this."

Kitty nodded. While Velma was busy cleaning up the mess, she'd call Aunt Gloria. "Hello, Aunt Gloria, it's me, Kitty."

"Kitty, I have so much to tell you."

"Me, too. For starters, the police have arrested Tracy Taylor Evan for the murder of Rich Evan. She's one of his ex-wives."

"Oh, dear," said Aunt Gloria. "That doesn't make sense. That doesn't make any sense at all."

"What do you mean?"

"I found out about this Barbados nut. It's also known as kukui haole. There are only a few places where it grows from what I gather. The nearest one to California is Hawaii. Was Tracy in Hawaii recently?"

"Kukui haole? Hawaii? I have no idea. She might have been. I'm sure the police will check it out." Hawaii? Why did that sound familiar to her?

"And that house!" cried Aunt Gloria, excitedly. "Kitty, you'll never believe what I found out!"

Jack looked at the clock on the dash and cursed. It was five minutes fast and no matter how he computed it, time was running out. One hand on the wheel, the other gripping his phone, he tried for the hundredth time to reach Kitty on her cellphone.

He cursed. Busy again!

"The Wright house does have the most intriguing history, just as you described, Kitty." Aunt Gloria was talking animatedly. "So many odd occurrences and murders."

"Don't tell me you want to blame Rich Evan's death on evil spirits, too, Aunt Gloria?"

Aunt Gloria said no. "Kitty, do you remember you told me about a Bruce Churchill?"

"Sure, he blew his brains out."

"That's right. And his lover was a man and he went crazy and spent the rest of his life in an insane asylum."

"I know all that," said Kitty, somewhat disappointed that Aunt Gloria hadn't been more helpful.

"But, Kitty," said Aunt Gloria sotto voce, "did you know that Churchill's lover was your bestfriend's grandfather?"

Kitty's heart screeched to a halt. "What?" Her head was shaking. "Churchill's lover was Velma's grandfather? That's impossible. The man that had been living with Churchill at the Wright house was named Kresge. And Velma only has one set of grandparents. Her father was an orphan. She told me so."

Aunt Gloria interrupted her. "Yes, I've researched all that. But Velma's grandmother is actually Humphries-Kresge."

"But—"

230

"Her maiden name was Humphries. I guess she went back to it after her husband left for California."

"But that would mean—"

"It means," warned Aunt Gloria, "that you'd better be very careful."

Hawaii? Velma had recently been to Hawaii. Velma said she wheedled the trip out of her grandmother when she graduated from the culinary institute. And if Velma had been in Hawaii—

Kitty heard the sound of somebody clearing their throat and turned with a start. Velma stood framed in the kitchen doorway. There was a long and mean looking butcher's knife in her fist.

Velma was smiling madly. "Hang up the phone, Kitty."

Kitty bit her lip and dropped the telephone. "Wha-what are you doing, Velma? What's going on?"

Velma took a step towards Kitty. "You can come out now!"

Kitty turned as the bedroom door creaked open. "Gil," she gulped, "Major?"

Velma waved the big knife through the air. Velma was a trained chef. She was good with a knife. Kitty vowed to keep her distance.

Gil, however, had no such qualms, and he wrapped his arms around Velma and planted a big kiss on her cheek.

Velma said, "Katherine Karlyle meet Gil Evan."

Kitty blanched. "Evan? You mean, you're related to Rich Evan?" What on earth was going on here? And whatever it was, how was she ever going to get out of it alive? Had Aunt Gloria heard anything suspicious before Kitty had been forced to hang up the telephone? And would it do any good if she had?

Kitty groaned. If only she had told her aunt where she was calling from!

Gil grinned ear to ear. He bowed. "Rich Evan's long lost brother."

Kitty's mouth was dry. "Brother?"

"That's right," explained Velma. "You see, Rich and Gil are orphans, just like my dad was. That's what got this all started. I was looking up stuff about my dad, trying to find his family." She twirled the knife around her ear. "That's what got the wheels turning. I discovered that Rich Evan had an older brother. Gil is two years Rich's senior. Their parents were killed in an automobile accident. The boys were separated and went to live with foster parents."

Kitty nodded. She knew that Rich had been raised by foster parents. But, a brother!

"The Wright house is mine, you know."

"Yours?"

Velma's eyes darkened. "Bruce Churchill promised that house to Gramps. Poor Gramps. Left Michigan one day on a whim and never went back. Probably because he figured out he was gay. Of course, that was considered quite an embarrassment at the time."

"So he disappeared and your grandmother changed her name."

"That's right. But the Randalls were already in California and they had a soft spot for my grandmother and my grandfather, too. They gave him a job helping out, doing menial labor. That's when he met Bruce Churchill, a lawyer who was doing a bit of legal work for the Randalls."

"I am so sorry, Velma." Just keep her talking, thought Kitty. Show her some sympathy. Keep breathing. . .

"Just because Gramps went nuts is no reason to renege on a promise. But no," wailed Velma, "Churchill's family, they had good lawyers. Saw to it that Gramps was locked up and kept the house for themselves."

She grinned madly. "But I'm getting it back now. I'm the rightful owner. And I found Gil."

"I was working as a laborer back in England. Velma contacted me and made me an offer which, as you Americans say, I couldn't resist."

"I got Granny to recommend him for a job with the Randalls, since she's all buddy-buddy with them. After that, I set the wheels in motion."

"You killed Rich Evan?"

"Yeah. Didn't mean to, not right away, at least. I wasn't too sure about the kukui haole. The idea was to kill the dog first and test out the dosage. But," she said rather proudly, "the script changed when that fathead ate the food and died."

"Saved us some time and trouble," added Gil.

"You bet," said Velma.

"How did you get the poison in Benny's food? It was with me all the time until I went to Mr. Evan's house." Kitty decided the best strategy was to keep asking questions and pray that Gil and Velma would keep answering them. The longer the game was played, the longer she stayed alive.

"Rich liked to hang out at The Disco Den. I was waiting for him."

Kitty's eyes widened. "You slept with him the night he

died?" She glanced at Gil. Didn't the man mind that Velma had slept with his brother?

Things were getting clearer now. The address book. "You dropped the address book in your soup on purpose. You were afraid I'd find your name and address inside."

Velma clapped. "That's right. What are you looking so surprised about? You don't think a guy like Rich could go for a fat slob like me, is that it?"

"No," cried Kitty, "that's not it at all. I don't think you're any of those things!"

"Sure, Little Miss Perfect. Perfect parents, perfect life. Some of us haven't had it so easy."

Kitty was shaking her head. "It's not true. . ."

"Well, he liked me just fine. We partied at my place. The man was a walking drug store. I'm half-surprised he didn't kill himself driving home."

"I still don't see how Benny's food got tainted."

"I walked up to Rich's house from the beach. There's a public access along Pacific Coast Highway. The rich farts hate it, but it's there if you know where to look. I figured the way we'd been partying that Rich would be out of it and that I'd only have to wait for that housekeeper of his to be out of the way. Then his ex-wife comes by and snatches the dog."

Velma's hands tightened around the handle of the knife. "I could have killed her."

That explained the sunburn Velma had the day poor Mr. Evan had died. Velma had blamed it on gardening without sunscreen or a hat, instead she'd been marching up the beach on her way to a murder.

Kitty wondered if she could make it to the front door

before Velma caught her.

"But then I saw you coming with Benny's precious lunch and I decided to go through with the plan. I mean, I didn't know Tracy was thinking of stealing the damn dog, I only thought she was taking it for a ride somewhere."

"And then Rich ate the food and I got the blame."

Gil and Velma laughed together. "Yeah, that was a hoot," Velma said.

"You killed Mrs. Randall, too, didn't you? Why? What did she do to you?"

"Oh," said Velma, "that was your fault, Kitty."

"My fault?" Velma was mad. Mad like her grandfather had been. Was it hereditary?

"Don't you remember? It was all that spiritualist stuff. If you hadn't gone poking around, sticking your nose into things that were none of your business." Velma jabbed the knife in Kitty's direction and Kitty jumped.

"You got Mrs. Randall thinking about Bruce Churchill and Gramps. What if she put two and two together? What if she had figured out that I was involved in all this?"

"I had to kill her. I would have killed her husband, too, if he'd been home. Just my luck the man was out of town."

Kitty felt chilled to the bone and still she was sweating. Where was all this anger and bitterness that Velma held coming from?

Velma handed Gil the knife. Kitty stole a look at the front door. "Don't even think about it," Gil said cruelly.

"What's going to happen now?" Kitty asked. "What are you going to do to me?"

"What's going to happen now," Velma called from the

kitchen, "is that in a month or so Gil Evan, Rich's long lost brother, will be found. And he'll inherit everything. Did I tell you we're getting married?"

Kitty didn't answer.

Velma reappeared. Her hands held a bowl. She smiled. "Have some soup."

# 32

"I-I'm really not hungry." Kitty backed towards the wall.

Velma followed her. "Come on, Kitty, try it. It's my own recipe. I think you'll like it." She held the steaming bowl aloft, grinning evilly.

Kitty slowly shook her head.

Velma's voice took on a hard edge. "Come on, Kitty. Drink the soup. Believe me, it's easier this way. You wouldn't rather have the knife, would you?"

Velma grabbed Kitty's arm and twisted it roughly behind her back. Kitty howled. Velma pushed the soup to her mouth. Hot, poisonous soup splashed over Kitty's face and scalded her tongue. She gagged. Velma was pushing her to the floor.

The door flew open. Jack burst in. "Kitty, are you okay?"

Velma screamed in frustration and tossed the bowl at the

detective. He dodged to one side. The bowl missed him, but not the knife that Gil had thrown. Jack hadn't seen it coming. It struck him in the thigh and he went down.

"Jack!" Kitty shouted in horror. Velma had released her grip on Kitty and she scrambled to Jack's aid. Gil lunged at the fallen detective, grabbed the knife and was about to hit him with it again when Jack managed to pull out his revolver. He shot once and Gil went down on top of him.

The explosion shattered Kitty's ears. And the air was filled with dancing stars. She heard moaning and didn't know if it was Jack or Gil or both of them.

Kitty struggled to her feet and turned toward the sound of footsteps. "Velma!"

A long deboning knife glistening in Velma's fist. Kitty was going to be sliced to ribbons. She grabbed a cushion and threw. Foam peanuts exploded all around as Velma's knife slashed through the material.

"Velma, please,"begged Kitty. "It doesn't have to be like this."

"You are such a pain," hissed Velma. "Look at the trouble you've caused." She dove.

Kitty snatched a lamp off the table and wrapped her hands around it. She closed her eyes. If she was going to die, she was going to go down swinging.

Her hands shook and the lamp fell from her grasp. She'd hit something! Kitty opened her eyes. Velma looked dazed. But she was still coming, blood oozing from her temple.

Kitty reached for the broken lamp. Velma's knife dug into her arm and she recoiled. Burning pain shot through her arm and raced all the way to her shoulder. She kicked.

Velma kicked back and she was bigger and stronger. "Stop struggling, bitch!"

Velma flipped Kitty over on her back. She straddled Kitty with her big legs on each side, effectively anchoring her victim down. Kitty was going to be pinned to the floor! Blindly, Kitty lashed out with her arms. Her hand found the lamp and she slammed it against Velma's ear.

Velma squealed with rage. She grabbed her ear and bounced up and down on Kitty a couple of times. Kitty could barely breathe. And she'd dropped her weapon.

The deboning knife was only inches from her eyes and coming fast. Kitty squeezed her eyes shut. Her mind went blank. This was it. This was Death. Hardly the way she'd pictured it.

A large boom shook the room. Kitty opened her eyes. Velma was falling off to one side. Her other side was covered with blood. The deboning knife fell harmlessly to the carpet. Kitty pulled herself out from under Velma's weight.

"Jack! Are you okay?"

The detective laid his revolver on the ground. Gil was still clinging to him, even in death. "So," said Jack, "some third date, eh?"

# 33

Jack limped into the kitchen. Libby was trailing along behind, wagging her tail.

"How's your leg?" Kitty asked.

"I won't be doing any dancing for a couple of months, but otherwise it's not so bad. How's your arm?"

Kitty involuntarily winced, remembering the way Velma had stabbed her in the upper arm—the same arm that now brandished a cheap plastic spatula she'd found in one of his kitchen drawers. "Better. Where'd you get this thing, anyway?" She waved the white spatula in front of his nose. "One of those dollar stores?"

He grinned and helped himself to a glass of water. "Better still. The bargain bin at the dollar store. Three for a dollar. I got a can opener and a pizza cutter, too." He started rummaging around in the drawer. "They're in here somewhere."

Kitty rolled her eyes.

"Hey, they work great."

"So what happened?" Kitty broke open a half dozen eggs and dropped them into a large glass bowl. Libby's tail went crazy.

"Not much. Velma won't stop talking. In fact, she's rather proud of herself."

"The poor girl. She must be insane. I hope she gets help."

"She tried to kill you, Kitty!"

Kitty shrugged. "I can't help it. She was my friend."

"You're a little crazy yourself. You know that?" Jack sat at the small kitchen table and looked out the back window. "The funny thing is, it looks like Velma Humphries is going to end up spending the rest of her days at the Hollywood Hills Psychiatric Hospital once she recuperates."

"Like her grandfather?"

"Just like her grandfather. Weird, isn't it?"

Kitty nodded. It was too weird. There was something very strange about the Wright house and she was very glad to have no reason to ever return there.

"Oh, I don't think you'll be delivering meals to Richard Couric and Timothy Toms for a while."

"What's happened?"

"They've flown the coop, as the saying goes. Put the house up on the market. Looks like they'll be setting up shop elsewhere. They must have been feeling too much heat."

Kitty nodded. It was probably for the best. "And I had a call from Tracy. She was so excited. She's gotten a six-week engagement opening for a magic act in Vegas."

"I guess all the publicity did her more good than bad."

"That's what she said. I'm happy for her." Kitty unwrapped a hunk of meat wrapped in foil. "The odd thing is that Fang Danson and Angela Evan still want me to cook meals for Benny and Little Rich."

"Go figure." Jack tilted his glass and watched Kitty grating some sort of cheese. "You going to do it?"

"Of course. I have a business to run."

"You could run it from here." In response to Kitty's puzzled look, Jack added, "From my house."

"We are *not* married, Jack."

He rose and looked over her shoulder. "It's only a matter of time. Right, Lib?"

The Labrador barked once.

"See? Lib knows." He sniffed. "What's that you're cooking? Some sort of an omelet?"

Kitty gave Jack her best smile. "Oh, not just an omelet. I've named this recipe especially for you."

"Really?" Jack sounded pleased.

"Yep, I call this the My True Jack Omelet."

Jack wrapped a hand around Kitty's waist for support. His leg was throbbing. "With cheese?"

"Yes," Kitty quipped, pointing to the saucer of grated cheese, "a little jack," she lifted the meat from the cutting board, "and a *lot* of *ham*."

Also available from Beachfront

# IT'S A YOUNG, YOUNG WORLD
by Glenn Meganck

*"It's A Young, Young World by Glenn Meganck is the story of an aging American senator and his compatriots who are mysteriously drawn by a scientist's dying words about the secret of eternal youth and the ability to live forever. Struggling to keep up in a youthful world, retiring Senator Chauncy and his 20-something bride purse an opportunity to recapture the power and excitement of youth in this fast-paced, wryly told, deftly written adventure laced with a very special insight into today's youth-centric culture. **Highly recommended.** "* Midwest Book Review

It's a young world and Senator Robert Chauncy is old and getting older. Soon to be retired, the senator and his young bride are off to Florida for a little honeymoon. But his wife, Sheila, has a wandering eye and Fate has other surprises for them as well. On their way down the eastern seaboard, Sen. Chauncy finds himself trying to rescue a drowning man. The stranger dies, but before passing away, he baffles the senator and the gathered spectators with a mad tale of living forever. At first, his words are taken for those of a man in caught in delirium. But it is soon discovered that the seemingly middle-aged dead man was in reality an eccentric and elderly foreign scientist named Titus Olshenski. Sen. Chauncy and the others begin to wonder if Olshenski's dying words carry some hidden meaning. Did Olshenski have the key to the Fountain of Youth? Can the scientist's riddle be unlocked? Can they find the Fountain of Youth? Fate only knows, and before long, the race is on to see who will live forever and who is doomed to die.

*"Exceptional!!!"* Today's Books

Join Sen. Chauncy, who longs to be virile enough to satisfy his young wife; an aging hippy named Rocky and his own wife, Laura, with disabling multiple sclerosis;  a puzzling and disturbing old man whose motives are unknown; a young lifeguard with the hots for the senator's wife; an old woman and her cat, Lester; a vain former teen idol who craves a return to his glory days and the rest of the zany cast as they race to be the first to the Fountain of Youth in Glenn Meganck's fast, fun and furious adventure, IT'S A YOUNG, YOUNG WORLD, a story that explores the power and allure of youth in today's culture and the extreme effort some will exert to maintain or regain their own youthfulness in the face of growing old.

www.GLENNMEGANCK.COM

# BUM RAP IN BRANSON

a Tony Kozol mystery

by J.R. Ripley

"Taken separately, the elements that make up this seventh Tony Kozol novel might sound downright goofy. Country musician Kozol and his pal Rock Bottom are hired to play at "Kewpiecon," a Kewpie doll convention in Branson, Missouri. While there, they befriend--and defend--real-life country singer Jim Stafford, who stands accused of murdering rapper B.A.D. Spike. Spike, who was opening a controversial theater in Branson, has plenty of enemies--but Stafford is found standing over the body. When Kewpie merchandise is stolen and a conventioneer is murdered, new suspects emerge. From descriptions of the bizarre antics of the Kewpie conventioneers to the quirky characterization of Stafford (who older country fans will remember for his hit "Spiders and Snakes"), **Ripley spins a truly funny yarn that will have readers laughing out loud. An offbeat hit** that will appeal especially to country music fans." —Booklist

"**A delightfully funny mystery novel!**" Susan K. Scott
President-Bonniebrook Historical Society

"J. R. Ripley's Bum Rap In Branson is an exciting mystery novel featuring Tony Kozol and Rock Bottom, who is drawn into a bizarre recurrence of Kewpie dolls and murders, their interconnection unknown. The latest entry in a genuinely thrilling series, Bum Rap In Branson complicates Tony's desire to just get by, have fun, and earn a few bucks playing the guitar by saddling him with a murder accusation - he has to clear his name fast to avoid singing in jail! **A viciously delightful read for mystery/suspense enthusiasts!**"
—Midwest Book Review


"**Must read!**" — Today's Books, A Public News Service

CeeCee Kewpie has been placed in the Witness Protection Program and is believed to be living under an assumed name in the American Southwest.

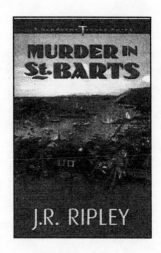

MURDER IN ST. BARTS

a Gendarme Charles Trenet novel

by J.R. Ripley

An exciting new series by the critically acclaimed author of the Tony Kozol mysteries. Murder and romance fill the air on the exotic island of St. Barts in the French West Indies...

"It would be hard not to like Murder In St. Barts. The dialogue, the humor, and the sarcasm give us all something to enjoy." I Love A Mystery

"Trenet is a well-developed, likable character, and the novel offers an absorbing mystery set in the exotic playground of the rich and famous. An entertaining new series..." Booklist

Look for upcoming Beachfront releases by featured authors including Marie Celine, Nick Lucas, Glenn Meganck,  J.R. Ripley and more!

Beachfront Publishing

"Independent Books for Independent Minds."

Beachfrontentertainment.com